King of the Streets, Queen of His Heart 4

A Legendary Love Story

PORSCHA STERLING

They conquer...

Chapter One

LEGEND

"I'mma blast every fuckin' body up in this bitch, I put dat shit on everything," Murk grumbled as he scowled at the older Black cop who was standing in front of the metal cage we were in, watching us with an evil ass grin on his face.

Standing up, Murk flicked him a bird and gritted on him, showing his mouth full of gold teeth.

"The fuck you lookin' at, you field niggin' ass muthafucka!" he snapped at the cop who, in return, grunted before turning to walk away. "That's right. Get yo' muhfuckin' ass out of here before I blast you in yo' shit."

"With what gun, nigga? Just sitcho ass down somewhere and wait for Blitzstein to come get us," Dame laughed coarsely, as he looked at Murk who had begun pacing back and forth in the cell.

"And what the hell is field niggin'?" I asked, slightly amused at the way Murk was going off, although I was starting to get a little agitated myself.

We'd been locked up a few times, but this was the first time that we didn't get right back out in only a couple hours. I knew that Shanecia had called Blitzstein who was a beast as a lawyer, but he was taking a long ass time and it was starting to fuck with me a bit. We needed to get out this bitch because we had shit to do, things to handle, and people to see.

"I called him a field niggin' ass muthafucka because his ass over here workin' overtime for massa," Murk grumbled as he finally took a seat. "Of all the fuckin' things he can do and he wanna bring his black ass over here to watch us!"

"I'm just tryin' to figure out what the hell is taking Blitzstein so long," Dame said, as he stood up and walked to the front of the cell and peered out.

Lifting one brow, I watched him but I was more in tuned to what was going on in my mind than what he was doing. The fact that they'd arrested everyone but Quan told me that this was obviously something to do with the night that I'd killed Mello, and Quentin had taken care of the FBI chick. It was also clear that they had a decent amount of evidence on us to know that Quan hadn't been there when that incident happened. But we'd been too careful to leave anything behind, so that had to mean that somebody snitched. But who?

"Quentin," I said as soon as the question came to my mind.

"Huh?" Dame asked from beside me. "What about Quentin?"

I shook my head softly. This wasn't the place to speak about those things. The whole reason they locked us up together and made us sit

2

for hours was probably to make us speak, so we could talk our ass into giving up the evidence they needed. I wasn't that damn stupid. They would have to come with something else.

When I looked up, I locked eyes with Murk and he gave me a subtle nod of the head. I knew right then that he had been thinking the same damn thing I was thinking: Quentin had to be the snitch.

"Last time I was locked up, they had some big ass bitch in the holding cell with me. They said it was a man, but I swear that nigga was a bitch. His name was Benji and she...he, hell, I'll say 'shim'. 'Shim' kept scratching his junk and sniffing its fingers. Ever since then, I get anxiety and shit when I get behind bars," Dame explained with a stressed expression on his face.

After eyeing his soft ass, I glanced over at Murk and we both burst out laughing.

"Nigga, *that's* why you think you get anxiety from being locked up? Because of Becky-Benji?" Murk said in between chuckles.

"Y'all ain't shit," Dame replied, cutting his eyes at the both of us. "I was fucked up seeing that shit. They kept me in the cell for two hours, watching that bitch pace back and forth and sniff his fuckin' stank ass fingers. I just knew he was gone try to touch me and I'd have to kill his ass...then I woulda caught me another case. I got post-traumatic stress disorder about that shit!"

"Dame, spell post-traumatic stress disorder," Murk shot back, still laughing his ass off as Dame glared at him.

"Nigga, it's spelled P-T-S-D...post-traumatic stress disorder," Dame replied back, looking at Murk like he was the dumbest person

3

on Earth. "You don't know about that shit? It's when something fucked up happens to you and—"

"Muhfucka, I know what the fuck it is. I'm sayin' yo dumb ass don't have that shit," Murk responded while laughing at the look on Dame's face.

"Y'all some fools," I said, laughing at the two of them going back and forth.

Then we all stopped talking when we heard the sound of hurried feet approaching. Two plain-clothed agents walked by the cell, talking amongst themselves.

"Kayla said that some pregnant chick in a wedding dress is about to attack Cheryl, so we gotta walk out front and make sure her and her friend don't do no stupid shit," one of the agents said.

"I still got three minutes left on my damn break. Why the hell she ain't call somebody else to—"

"Pregnant chick in a wedding dress?" Murk repeated as soon as they walked through the door to the other part of the building. "Aw, shit. That's probably Li."

"And she got Neesy out there with her. They raising hell, huh?" I said with a smile on my face, happy with that fact that Shanecia was here for me instead of somewhere ready to catch a flight back to Atlanta.

"Fuck…Li might get her ass locked up in this bitch. She don't have a shred of gotdamn sense," Murk grumbled as he sat down and shook his head.

"Well, that means you married the right one because neither do you," Dame joked, and Murk punched him in his side.

Stuffing my hands in my pocket, I closed my eyes as a smile crossed my face. My baby was here and she was fighting to get me out this bitch.

Shanecia just might love a nigga for real.

Chapter Two

SHANECIA

"Listen, this how this shit is going to go. Wait…you listening? I need to make sure you really hear me…Cheryl," Maliah added after checking the name plaque on top of the desk ahead of her.

I watched as Maliah leaned over the top and stared down at the butch looking white officer, who returned her glare without answering.

"You need to give me some muthafuckin' answers! Y'all came and grabbed my new husband up hours after we got married and I need to know why!" she shouted at the woman.

"Ma'am, I'm going to have to ask you to step back and to calm down—"

"You don't need to ask me to do shit because I'm not doing shit until I get some gotdamn answers. Now why did you arrest them?"

Stepping up, I crossed my arms in front of my chest, acutely aware of the fact that nearly every one of the FBI agents standing in the front office area we were in was looking right at us.

As soon as they tucked Legend, Murk and Dame in the back of

their SUV and drove off, Maliah and I took off after it and followed it all the way here. The last thing that was going to happen was that they take them somewhere and deliver their own kind of justice and kill all three of them in retaliation for losing one of their own.

"We aren't leaving until you tell us where they are! You aren't about to kill them and then act like it was some muthafuckin' accident. I know how y'all roll," I added with a frown.

The white woman pursed her lips while bringing her brows forward to create a hood over her eyes as she glared at me. But I didn't care. One thing I was not going to do was leave. I'd done that before when Legend needed me but he was my fiancé now, which meant that she'd have to drag my ass up out of here before I left.

I heard the sound of someone clearing her throat and I turned towards the noise, instantly locking eyes with the pretty Black woman who had arrested them. She was about my complexion, a cool chestnut brown, with high cheekbones and large doe-like, oval eyes. She had soft hair that was braided into goddess braids and pulled into a crown on the top of her head. But that is where the softness stopped. Her eyes were hard and penetrating, and she stood with her shoulders squared in a way that told you she wasn't one to be fucked with.

However, I wasn't the least bit afraid of her and neither was Maliah. I turned and, with my hands on my hips, stared straight back at her, waiting for her to give me an explanation on what was going on with Legend and his brothers.

"I'm Special Agent Martinez. Your *friends*..." she started, which made me frown. I didn't like the way she said 'friends' in such a callous and demeaning way. "…have been arrested for the murder of a Federal agent. You won't be able to see them until I decide to let them go. But don't hold your breath on that happening."

"And what evidence do you have that says my *husband* and his brothers murdered someone?" Maliah added, looking the woman up and down as she put extra emphasis on the word husband.

The woman's eyes shined and a chilling smirk crossed through the cruel expression on her face.

"We have enough, and they will pay for what they've done, believe that," she threatened in a chilling tone. "They are responsible for killing more people in the southern region of this state than any group I've ever known. They are *terrorists*! Now get the fuck out of my building!"

"Bitch, I'll—"

"Wait!" I tugged on Maliah's arm to stop her from going in. The last thing I needed was for her to get locked up and then I have something else to deal with. "Blitzstein is on this so let him handle it. I'll call him to see what's going on. Just calm down. You got the babies to think about and besides…" I stared at the woman up and down with the deadliest look I could give her, hoping it would disintegrate her ass right where she stood. "…this uptight, broke, stick-up-the-ass bitch ain't even worth it."

Grabbing Maliah by the arm, I pulled her out of the glass front doors as Agent Martinez stared us down, her eyes cut so narrowly, it was a wonder to me that she could even see. Her eyes spewed pure hatred at us, and it rattled me to the core. I could tell that she was hell-bent on making Legend, Murk and Dame go down for murder, and even though I didn't know what kind of evidence she had, I had a feeling that it was enough.

*****

"This is not going to be easy," Blitzstein started, and I instantly held my breath as I gripped the phone in my hand. "I can get them out because it's against the law for them to hold them much longer. But you have to realize that they are being held for murdering an FBI agent. So every single thing they can do to stop me from getting them out is being done. The police…the judges…all these people work together and they don't take it kindly when someone murders their own. It'll be an uphill battle from here."

Biting my bottom lip, I glanced at Maliah who was sitting to my side, still wearing her soiled wedding dress. It was the next day and we were still outside the FBI building, unwilling to leave until we heard something. I had a bad feeling about the whole ordeal but, on top of everything, I was worried sick, and the only thing keeping me in check was knowing that I was somewhere close to where Legend was. I couldn't go home, couldn't eat and couldn't sleep, until I saw him walk up out of there.

"What kind of evidence do they have on them?" I asked, more worry lines popping up on my forehead. Maliah sat beside me, wiping at her eyes, and I knew she was crying. The fire in her had cooled, and now the sadness and grief was pouring through.

"That's the thing…they aren't being forthcoming with it so that usually means they are protecting someone or something. They must have an informant," Blitzstein continued.

Chills ran up and down my spine. Who could have told on them? Ever since what happened with Alpha, Legend had made it so they kept all important information amongst themselves and rarely trusted others to do their dirty work. I loved that he took the extra precautions, but it saddened me that it always kept him away from home so much to handle business.

"That's the bad news, but we will deal with that later. Right now, I just want to get them out and it looks like I'll be able to do that. They just need to lay low and be careful because the FBI will be watching for any reason to bring them back in on some bullshit just so they can keep them locked up," he told me.

"Thank you," I replied graciously.

A tear came to my eye, but I blinked it away and tried to focus on the fact that Legend would be in my arms soon. For how long, I didn't know. But I would cherish each second of it, and I'd fight to keep it that way.

Hanging up the phone, I turned to look at Maliah who had sat down on the hood of Legend's G-Wagon. Her dress was hiked up, exposing her thick legs as she cradled her slightly rounded belly in her arms and sat quietly, seemingly deep in thought.

"I can't do this without him," she finally tearfully said, as I approached her and sat down on the hood beside her. "I know I talk a lot about shit about Murk because he ain't shit most times, but I love his ass. I can't live without my baby."

Reaching out, I cradled her in my arms as she cried against my chest. Pushing my own fears of being without Legend away, I rocked her back and forth and tried to get her to calm down. She needed me so I had to focus on helping her.

"You can live without him, Li-Li," I told her, speaking honestly. "You can do it, but let's pray that you won't have to."

Chapter Three

LEGEND

"Y'all can't keep looking out there," Dame told us. "It ain't gone do no good. It's just gonna fuck with your mind."

I heard him but I didn't move and neither did Murk. The cops had moved us into another cage. It was smaller and there was a window that gave us a view of the parking lot. They were fucking with us. They knew that we could see Shanecia and Maliah, so this was their form of playing mind-games with us.

What they didn't understand was the type of niggas they were dealing with. This shit didn't break us. Watching our ladies cry only made us more determined to get the fuck out of here so we could blast every single pig or snitch who was responsible for putting us here. The black chick with the smug look on her face would be first.

"I'mma kill these muthafuckas with a fuckin' smile on my face," Murk gritted as he watched Maliah cry while Shanecia held her in her arms.

My eyes were focused on Shanecia. The woman I'd finally bowed on one knee to in order to make her officially mine. As soon as we got out this bitch, I was wifing her ass up. I didn't need a big ceremony with a bunch of people around. I just wanted her to be mine.

Looking at her made me love her even more. She had to be devastated. I knew she was because I'd seen it all over her face while she was talking on the phone. But true to the selfless person she was, she was tending to her cousin instead of herself. I loved everything about that woman and it was fucking with me that I'd put her in a position where she was more inclined to cry than smile. Once I made it out of here, I would try my hardest to never make her cry again.

"It must be y'alls lucky day," an icy, feminine voice said from behind me.

I gritted my teeth and instantly felt the singe of anger in my chest. I knew who it was before I'd even turned around. My glare hit her face and I could see her eyes waver, as if she was momentarily caught off guard by the intensity of my stare. She wasn't untouchable. I knew it and so did she. She may have the power in here, but once I was on the streets, she didn't stand a chance against me.

"It looks like regardless to the strings we've pulled to try to keep you here, someone has made the stupid decision to let you bail out... for now," she threatened, looking directly into my eyes. "Our case against you all is air tight so I'll be seeing you soon. In the meantime, stay in the city."

She strode away with confidence. As I watched her stride, I recognized her type immediately. She wore her uniform a couple sizes too big, but it still didn't cover up her curves and nice shape. Her lengthy hair was pulled tight into a bun and she didn't have on a stitch of makeup. She was going overboard trying to hide every bit of allure, femininity and sex-appeal that came natural to her because she wanted respect for the ones around her.

Women like her were always uptight, undersexed and overworked. But they were also incredibly focused when they had a goal in mind. She couldn't be won over by greed because she was ambitious to a fault. She would be a hard one to crack.

"She's gonna be at our ass as soon as we shake out this bitch," Murk grumbled from beside me, mirroring my exact thoughts.

"She is. But ain't shit we can't handle," I answered him. "First thing's first, let's figure out what we gonna do once we get the fuck outta here. Might as well get comfortable, you know they gone make our asses sit as long as we can before they let us go."

Dame nodded his head. His eyes were on me but I could tell his mind was elsewhere. And just that quickly, mine went from our present situation and back to Shanecia. Walking over, I stood up straight and peered out of the small window above us. She was sitting on top of the hood of my car and was talking to Maliah about something that had placed a smile on her face. Maliah was no longer crying and was listening intently to every word her cousin was saying.

Stay with me, baby, I begged her in my mind. *Stay with me and I'll make everything right.*

I had no idea what was going through Shanecia's mind right now, but I hoped she wasn't thinking about leaving again. I needed her. If she tried to leave me again, it would destroy me. There was no way I could let her go.

*****

Six hours later, we were finally released. They did every damn thing they could do in order to keep us in there, and I didn't blame them. If I were them, I would have wanted to lock my ass up for life too, because as soon as I got out that bitch, I had my mind set on wreaking havoc.

"Here are the last of your belongings. You're free to go," the clerk told me as she handed me over a bag with my phone and wallet inside.

The way her eyes lingered on my face as I placed my wallet in my pocket made me stop and look back up at her. I recognized the look in her eyes immediately. She had on her most serious fuck face but if she knew like I knew, she would step her ass to the side. The only woman I had on my mind was waiting for me on the other side of the double doors.

"Anything else I can help you with?" she asked me, her eyes silently telling me all the many things she would like to do.

"Yeah," I replied back as my eyes raked over her desk. "Your man buy you those?"

With her gaze suddenly filled with confusion, she squinted at me before letting her eyes fall on the bouquet of roses in a ceramic blue vase on top of her desk.

Shaking her head gently, she responded, "Yeah…well, I wouldn't call him *my* man but *a* man bought them for me."

Damn shame, I thought as I watched her lie so easily. I prayed for my sake and Shanecia's that she would never lie about some shit like this. She'd fuck around and get somebody killed over some stupid ass flowers.

"Lemme get one of them," I said without really asking, as I reached across and plucked one of the roses from the vase.

Before she could say anything, I turned and walked away towards where Murk and Dame were sitting by the door.

"You good?" Murk asked before letting his eyes drop to the rose in my hand. "Damn, why you ain't get me one for Li?"

He reached out to grab the rose but I batted his hand away with a smile on my face.

"Because you don't need this shit. You already wifed your broad up so she can't go nowhere for life. I'm still trying to help Neesy get her damn mind right," I informed him as Dame looked on.

"Well what about me, Legend? I just got Trell back," Dame said.

Murk and I both looked at him, each of us thinking the same damn thing.

"Nigga, if Trell can forgive you for all the shit you've done to her, ain't no jail time gone keep her ass away. She down with a nigga fo' sho'," I told him while shaking my head.

Dame smiled and looked away, obviously imagining Trell in his mind's eye. "Yeah, she fucks with me the long way. She done blessed my no good ass for sho' by coming back to a nigga, too. I can't lose her again."

Suddenly, the sound of heels clicking on the white tile floor erupted from behind us, and we all turned to see who was walking towards us. I wasn't the least bit surprised when I saw who it was.

"Well, look who it is. Agent Martinez," Dame said as he stepped forward and glared at her.

I didn't say a word but my eyes said plenty, and I could tell that she understood every word. She stood down the hall and watched as another agent, a man with a large, protruding belly and a bald head, walked over and unlocked the door for us. She continued to glare and I held her gaze as I backed out of the door, following behind Murk and Dame. Holding a smug smirk on my face, I rounded the corner and my eyes fell on Shanecia, who I could see waiting with Maliah on the other side of the glass building. As soon as I pushed open the door, she rushed out and jumped right into my arms.

"Damn, Neesy, you missed a nigga, huh?" I asked her as she nearly covered my whole face with kisses.

"No, I missed my fiancé," she corrected me then pulled back and flashed me the ring I'd placed on her finger the night before.

"Well, let me get you home so we can celebrate. I been missin' that ass," I told her while reaching back to give her lil' ole booty a squeeze.

She shot me a teasing smile and then gently pulled my hand from where it was…still cuffing her ass. I frowned as she laced her fingers through mine and pulled them down by our sides.

"What's up with you? You bashful all of a sudden and don't want your fiancé grabbing on that lil' tater tot you got back there, gul?" I joked with her, loving the way she cut her eyes at me. She hated when I talked about her little ass but, hell, I loved it and I loved her, so the shit was hilarious to me.

Grabbing the door, she jumped inside of the car but before she closed it shut, a flicker of light passed through her eyes, cluing me in to her evil intent.

"I hope you're enjoying yourself and that lil' grab you got because we're going to be celibate up until we get married."

As soon as she let that bullshit fall out of her mouth, she slammed the door closed and stared back at me with a look that said 'checkmate', but she had another thing coming.

"I'mma ignore that bullshit you accidentally said," I muttered after I sat down on the driver's side of the car.

"I didn't accidentally say anything. I really mean that, Legend! I heard that it will help us create boundaries before we get married so there is something to look forward to. And, we'll be closer as a couple."

I could feel my eyes bulging out of my head as she spoke to me. She must have thought that I was some nigga named Charles that she'd met down at the college or some shit.

"Neesy, wherever the fuck you got that stupid shit from, you need to give it the fuck back. I didn't ask your ass to marry me so you could start rationing off the pussy. What the fuck you thinking?"

She grumbled something under her breath but I ignored her, as I shifted the car into gear and pulled out of the parking lot.

"Now when we get home, I'm takin' a shower and I expect to come out and see you face down ass up, just like a nigga like it." I licked my lips and smirked as she cut her eyes at me, just because I knew I was getting on her last nerves. She wouldn't be mad for long. She had to know I wasn't going for that shit.

"But Legend, I planned for us to—"

"Like I always say," I started, cutting her off. "The good thing about having a plan A is that there is always a muthafuckin' plan B when you find out you was planning on doing some dumb shit! Now gone ahead and do them kimbels or whatever it's called that you chicks do to get that shit tight when you wanna give a nigga some."

I almost made myself choke trying to hold back my laughter and keep a straight face. Although I was looking straight ahead, I could feel the wind from how fast Shanecia had whipped her head around to glare at me. If looks could kill, she'd be pushing my ass out of the car into the ditch on the side of the road.

"Kimbels?! You mean *kegels*?" she asked and I shrugged. She knew what the hell I meant.

"I don't need to do that. That's an exercise to keep it tight and I don't have no issues in that department." She clicked her tongue in a cocky way that made me smile.

"Well, when we get to the house, I'm going to go down there and check it out for myself," I replied.

Glancing at her, I lifted one brow up and gave her a stern stare.

"It's a big job but I'm man enough to do it."

Rolling her eyes, Shanecia folded her arms at her chest, as I was so used to her doing, and sucked her teeth before looking out the window.

"I hate your ass, I swear," she told me.

Chuckling, I replied back, "I love you too."

Chapter Four

MALIAH

"Gotdaaaaaamn, Murk," I exhaled breathlessly as Murk slid out of me slowly, spreading the last remains of his seed on the inside of my thigh. Grabbing a towel from the nightstand, he wiped it up and then gave me a look that had me ready to go again.

That federal bitch had fucked up our wedding night but not for long. And as much as she thought she was going to keep us in the city, she wasn't stopping our honeymoon either. We were back at the house for now, but Murk assured me that as soon as he was able to finish handling some business, we would be on a plane to celebrate our new life together. I, for one, couldn't wait, and I hoped he didn't take too long to get things together because I only had a few months left before I wouldn't be able to fly.

"Yo' shit gushy as fuck. Don't tell me you missed me," he said with a teasing smile, as he stood up while biting down on his bottom lip.

"Naw, I ain't miss yo' ugly ass," I shot back with my own joke.

Stopping, he turned around and looked at me with a cocky smile on his face.

"I done been a lot of thangs, shawty, but I ain't never been ugly. Just be happy you locked a nigga down because the hoes be flocking."

I rolled my eyes and slid sideways so I could stand up and walk into the bathroom with him to clean up. That cocky arrogance ran in the Dumas family. The twins would probably have a head big as their daddy when they came out.

"Nigga, flock yo' ass into the bathroom and clean my juices off your dick. Don't be talking about them hoes while you still got me all over your lips."

"Good point," he said.

Then he flicked his long tongue out and licked all around the outside of his lips in a way that made me almost have an orgasm just from watching. Within seconds, I had pulled him close and wrapped one leg around him, locking him in place and rubbing my mound against his pole that, fortunately, was still hard.

"Naw, ma," Murk laughed as he pulled away from me. "We can't do that right now. I gotta give your ass a break before you start crying about being sore and shit."

Cutting my eyes at him, I watched as he walked away and started the shower.

"Get in so I can clean yo' fat ass up." He smacked me hard on my back side and squeezed, while biting his bottom lip. I playfully pushed him away and tied my hair up to get in the shower. He was always fucking with me and then wondered why I stayed ready to jump on his lap.

After showering together, I stepped out of the bathroom feeling like a new woman. I was starting a new life. Not only was I married to the man of my dreams, but I was going to have his babies. To say I upgraded from Danny was an understatement. Being with Murk made me forget that I'd ever even wasted time waiting for Danny to become a real man.

"Aye, what's this?" Murk asked as I was drying off.

He'd jumped out before me so that I could stay in and let the water run over me. After the last couple days I had, wasn't anything more relaxing to me than having a nice, long shower after good sex. Unfortunately, what Murk had in his hand was about to mess all of that up.

"What, bae?" I asked, turning around to face him.

My bottom lip dropped when I saw he was holding the letter that Danny had written me. How he found it, I had no idea. I'd hidden it inside of an old coffee canister in the pantry. Out of all the places in the house, I thought it would be safest there because Murk only drank Hennessy in his coffee mug and he had never, since I met him, tried to cook a damn thing.

"How did you get that?" I inquired, trying to play it cool and rub oil on my body so I could get dressed.

Inside, my mind was racing. There wasn't anything really bad in the letter, but I didn't know how Murk would act about Danny stating that he was going to take me to court about seeing the kids. It was his right as a father, but I knew that Murk wouldn't see it that way.

"Stop worrying 'bout how I got it and worry 'bout whether or not

I'mma fuck yo' ass up for tryin' to hide it from me!" Murk shot back with his eyes narrowed into slits. Then he sighed, and his face fell along with his shoulders.

"Li, we supposed to be past this hidin' shit. You my wife. Why the fuck you think you can just hide shit from me like I don't need to know? I gave you my last name…that gotta mean somethin', don't it?"

Now that made me feel like shit. He was right. I married Murk and here I was, still putting him through the boyfriend/girlfriend games.

"I'm sorry, baby," I told him as my heart twisted in my chest.

"Don't be sorry, nigga. Be careful," he shot back, making me look up at him. He had a slick ass grin on his face and I couldn't help but smile. Leaning forward, I punched him dead in his chest.

"I'm not gone take it too hard on you because I know why you hid it, but don't do no shit like this again. I don't hide anything from you and you shouldn't hide shit from me. You know I'mma find out anyways," he finished, and I nodded my head.

He was right about that shit. Murk had a radar or something when it came to me. It was impossible for me to hide shit from him and that started the day I met him. He always seemed to stumble upon the truth, or show up just in time to find me in a fucked up situation.

"Now, about this letter…not happenin'," he said as he crumbled it up and stuffed it in his pocket. "I don't want that nigga around the kids. Ever."

"But Murk, I can't—"

"Well, I can! I can make sure we don't have to deal with his bitch ass. You want me to do that?"

Sitting down on the bed, I shook my head as tears came to my eyes. This was the elephant in the room that I tried to ignore about Murk every day, but it was also the reality that hit me at the worst of times.

Murk was a killer.

He was my husband who loved me, adored the kids, and made me feel like the luckiest woman in the world. But he still was *that nigga*. His name wreaked havoc in the streets. His name ignited fear when spoken. Yes, he was my man but above all, he was a D-Boy and he didn't have a problem with taking care of his problems by giving someone a permanent dirt nap. That side of him scared the fuck out of me so I tried not to think of it.

"I can handle it, baby," I told him, wiping at my eyes and knowing full well that I didn't have the slightest idea on how I would make this go away. If Danny did try to push me to let him see the kids, which was his right as their parent, there wasn't shit I could do.

"Good," was all Murk said, ending the conversation.

*****

Murk promised me that, when we got married, he would try harder to make it back home to sleep in the bed with me each night. So far, we weren't on the same page when it came to what 'night' meant. In my mind, 'night' meant 'when the sun went down and the street lights came on'. To Murk, 'night' was 'any time before the sun came back up'. Leave it to his ass to make his own rules.

So now it was almost midnight, and I was still lying in the bed waiting for him to get home so that I could go to sleep. It wasn't too hard to stay awake because the twins were nocturnal just like their father and, although they were rather sluggish during the day, they loved to do somersaults and jab the shit out of me all through the night.

Grabbing my phone, I decided to text Murk. My mind had been telling me to leave him alone because I knew he was working and I shouldn't bother him. But then I remembered that I was his wife now, and I had a right to at least know when my husband was coming home.

Where are you? I texted, feeling on edge.

It was funny how I felt more comfortable with Danny being out all night than I did with Murk doing the same. Maybe it was because when Danny was gone, I knew what his ass was doing. He was somewhere getting high as a kite on his own supply. Deep down, I knew Murk was working but it didn't stop the doubt that I felt. It didn't stop the insecurities that swarmed through my heart, or the subtle whispers in my mind that he could be entertaining another woman.

I'll be on my way soon, was all he said.

A feeling of panic surged through my body as I was hit with the sudden and frantic notion that I was being stupid for waiting at home in the bed for my brand new husband to come home to me, while he did whatever with whoever in the streets. Then suddenly, almost as if Murk could feel my emotions from wherever he was, miles away, another text pinged on the screen of my phone.

Chill.

Chill. Such a Murk thing to say. It annoyed me and relaxed me at the same time.

"I need to stop sitting up here in the fuckin' dark," I muttered to myself as I set the phone to my side. "Got me drivin' myself crazy."

Standing up, I rubbed my stomach and decided to walk to the kitchen to grab something to drink. As soon as I opened the door, the sound of movement in the hall made me jump. Reaching out, I grabbed out to my side and picked up a pair of scissors that were laying on top of the dresser, and held it out in front of me as I crept down the hall trying to figure out who the hell was in my house and how they'd gotten past the alarm.

When I turned the corner, a small light suddenly flicked on in the living room and my eyes landed on the source of the commotion. My mama. But what confused me was the fact that she was fully dressed, with her purse tucked under her arm and her heels in hand, as she picked up her keys from the table, turned the light back off, and eased her way to the front door.

"What the hell?" I said under my breath as she walked out and closed the door behind her.

Dropping the scissors on the table, I scurried to the door and peeked out just in time to see her jump into her car that was parked in front of the house, start it up and drive off down the road. Now what the hell was she up to? She had told me a while ago she wasn't meeting up with her secret lover anymore in the middle of the night but, from the looks of it, that was a damn lie.

I heard a door open and turned around just in time to see Murk walk in from the garage. I'd been so in my thoughts wondering what the hell Loretta was up to that I hadn't even heard the garage open or close.

"What your nosey ass doing looking out the damn window?" he asked as he walked towards me with a smirk on his face. "Don't tell me you missed a nigga that much."

With my face still curled up in confusion, I shook my head and walked over to where he stood.

"I just saw Loretta's nasty ass sneaking out the damn house again! She told me she wasn't doing these midnight booty calls no more."

Murk started laughing and then grabbed me up in his arms. I couldn't help but suck in a deep breath to make sure that I couldn't catch the scent of another woman on him. It was a shame but I'd been dumb for a man before, and I wasn't ready to repeat that shit again.

"Your mama is grown, Li. Stay the fuck out her business and let her do what she wants to do. She wanted to move back home, but you asked her to stay to help you with the kids…you can't do that and then tell her what to do," he reasoned with me.

"Yeah, yeah…sounds right," I told him, rolling my eyes.

Deciding to drop that subject for the time being, I pulled away and shifted to the next thing that was on my mind.

"Why were you out so late? I thought you said you were going to start coming home earlier."

"I did come home earlier…shit, it just hit midnight, Li. You want me to be home before the 6 o'clock news or some shit?" he asked with his brows knitted up in annoyance.

"Why you gettin' so defensive?" I asked him, frowning as well, and squaring off my stance as I placed my hands firmly on my hips. "Who were you with that got you upset at me for askin' about you being out so late?"

Murk's eyes pierced mine for a minute and I could see the wheels in his head turning. Then suddenly, his face broke and he started to laugh.

"I can't believe this shit," he grumbled as he turned to walk away from me. "Get the hell out of here with that bullshit, Li. Don't make another bitch's problems your problems."

I heard what he said, but I still wasn't done and I definitely wasn't satisfied with his answer.

"Murk, don't walk away from me! I'm not playin' with you!"

Running up behind him, I grabbed him by one of his shoulders and swung him around to face me. His eyes were laced with anger and his jaw was clenched tight. I could tell he was trying his hardest not to blow up at me, but I really didn't care. Things were different now and I wanted him to act that way.

If you allowed a nigga to treat you like you ain't shit, he would do it. And I'd be damned if Murk continued on acting like I didn't deserve to know what he was up to when he was supposed to be next to me in *our* bed.

"What the fuck you want, Li?" he asked, crossing his arms in front of his chest as he glared at me. "You want me to start fuckin' around on you so you got a reason to be mad?"

I winced at his words and tears came to my eyes. And that let me know that I didn't really believe that Murk was messing around on me. If I did, it wouldn't have been so difficult to hear.

"I want you to be home at a decent time! Is that so much for your wife to ask? I want to know when I can expect you home so that I know for sure you didn't get arrested…or killed! I want to know that you'll be back at a certain time so I don't spend all night panicking and worrying about where the hell you are, or trying to figure out will I be burying or bonding my husband out of jail tonight!"

As soon as the words left my mouth, I realized that what I felt for Murk was irrational at times, crazy most times and indescribable all the time…but it was pure. No matter how many times Danny had been gone all night, I never worried about when he was coming home. In fact, I slept better in the bed without him. With Murk, it was different. I worried about him whenever he wasn't with me and I always needed him near.

"I'm sorry, Li," he apologized with sincerity, his tone lighter than before, as he walked towards me and wrapped me in his arms. "You won't have those worries anymore."

Kissing me on the top of my head, he scooped me up in his arms as if I weighed the same as a feather, and walked me down the hall. I melted in his arms as the love I had for him took over my heart.

With his charges pending, I didn't know what our future was going to be, but I knew for certain that I wanted this moment to last forever.

Chapter Five

TANECIA

There wasn't a day that went by that I didn't think about Jenta. Crazy, right? As much as I hated her when I first realized she existed, it was like she haunted my thoughts. Maybe it was because her baby lived with us and, aside from a few of Darin's features that stuck out—mainly his huge ears—she looked exactly like her mama. She was such a beautiful happy baby.

Since she was born, I had pretty much assumed the role as a mother without Darin asking me to. I felt like I had to, based on what had happened to her mother and the last words that Jenta had told me. I didn't expect it, but being a mother seemed to come natural to me. Being around Jen was just as good for me as it was for her.

"Open wide!" I cooed as I pushed the spoonful of applesauce inside of Jen's mouth.

She smiled and giggled, making drool and applesauce drip down her chin. Using the spoon, I cleaned it from around her mouth and then wiped her face.

"Okay, I guess you're done," I said as she continued to smile at me, showing off her mouth full of gums. "Let me finish getting you ready for daycare."

As I picked her up to get her changed and cleaned up, Darin walked in from the back, right on time, with one of her outfits in one of his hands, and her tiny pink booties in the other.

"I can get her ready," he offered. "The new manager at the gym is pretty good so I'm not rushing to leave."

I shook my head softly and leaned over to give him a kiss on the cheek.

"No, I can get her together. I made your smoothie but I didn't pour it yet. Why don't you do that while I handle Jen?"

Holding Jen's wiggling body to my chest, I slid past him and he swatted me on the backside just as I pushed by. Our relationship had grown tremendously just in the short couple months that Jen had been born, and I was happy for the new 'no drama' lifestyle I had going for myself. We had our issues but at least I wasn't getting my ass beat every day. I didn't even miss the name brand clothing, the bundles, or the brand new foreign cars that Mello would let me drive.

Actually, that was a damn lie. I did miss *some of* the foreign cars because even though Darin had lent me a very nice Mercedes Benz to drive around town in, it was about five years old and didn't have some of the luxury amenities I was accustomed to. On top of that, the air condition took a good 15 minutes to really get started and the doors creaked when I opened them. But who was I to complain? If it wasn't for him giving me the car to drive, I wouldn't have shit.

"She's all dressed," I announced to Darin as I walked in from the back.

Darin took one look at Jen and shook his head. "No, she isn't. Not with all that thigh meat hanging out."

"Darin, she's a baby!" I rolled my eyes as I pulled at the hem of the short baby pink one-piece.

It had the cutest white lace ruffle skirt attached to it that matched perfectly with her pink and lace booties. She was the cutest and I loved her as if she were my own.

"Right. And she's also *my* daughter and I won't have her going out with her ass out like that," he said as he grabbed Jen away from me and took her back to the room to change her.

Something about the way that he firmly declared she was 'his daughter' rubbed me the wrong way. It was true. She was his daughter and she wasn't biologically mine, but I never treated her any differently. And truth was, when it came to doing things for her, Darin seemed to expect me to do it regardless to whether she was biologically mine or not.

"Now this is much better," Darin said as they walked from down the hall.

When I looked up, I saw him holding Jen up. She was wearing the same top but he'd place some pink pants over the bottom and stuffed the lace skirt inside. Covering my mouth, I couldn't help but laugh.

"Darin, you can't just stuff the skirt inside of those pants. You can still see the print of it through the pants," I told him as I pressed at the imprint the lace made through Jen's pants.

"Yeah, but I know what you *can't* see through them and that's my baby's thighs." He leaned over and kissed me. I returned his embrace and then leaned down to kiss Jen on her forehead as they started to leave.

"Darin," I called out, stopping him just as he'd opened the door.

"Yes, bay?"

"Do you have a problem with me making decisions for Jen just because I'm not her biological mother?" I queried, unable to stop myself before the words came out.

Darin's eyes rose to the ceiling for a minute before they shifted back to mine, and he shook his head 'no'. But it still bothered me that he had to think about it.

"No, I don't. Even if Jenta hadn't passed away, your role in Jen's life would still be the same whenever she's here with us. She should love and respect you as the woman who is there for her when her mother isn't around. And I think she does even though she's still a baby." Darin looked down at Jen who giggled right on cue.

I smiled as Darin walked out, delivering one last grin in my direction before closing the door behind him.

What he said sounded good, but it still didn't feel right to me. For some reason, I still felt like Darin was guarded when it came to me. Almost like he wanted to distance me from his daughter unless it was convenient to have me around. Although I'd said some hurtful things about Jenta before she'd passed, and I envied her for being able to carry her child and deliver her into the world safe and sound, I never reflected anything negative onto Jen. As much as I wanted to believe that Darin knew I only had good intentions when it came to his daughter, something wasn't right and I felt it, even though he always said the right things.

He didn't trust me.

*****

"I've decided that I want to get a job…or enroll in school, maybe," I told Darin, feeling somewhat uneasy about mentioning it.

I didn't really have a skill that would make it easy to find a job, and I wasn't really the college type like Shanecia either. But one thing for sure, I needed to get out of the damn house and do something. I couldn't keep leaning on Darin to support me, and my little savings had pretty much run dry. I didn't have a lot of options.

"That's cool, I think it's a good idea," he said, sitting down on the chair across from me.

"Good…but in the meantime, do you think that I could maybe help out at the gym?"

Darin looked at me while biting his lip as if he were trying to hold back his laughter.

"You want to work at a gym, Tan? I've never seen you sweat a day in your life…what the hell would you do?"

Shrugging, I looked at Jen as she crawled over to me, and tried not to be offended. It seemed like all day I was looking in the classifieds and on the job posting sites, and seeing a bunch of shit I wasn't qualified for. Now, here Darin was reminding me how I wasn't even qualified to work at his gym and do what his other employees did: walk around, hand out towels and tell people where the locker room was.

"It's not like I want to be a personal trainer, Darin! I can at least work the floor."

"That's true, bay. My bad, I didn't mean to hurt your feelings. I was just sayin', you're not really the gym type like—"

I looked up in time to see Darin snap his mouth shut. An uneasy look crossed his face.

"Like who?" I pushed, feeling a funny feeling course through my chest. "Like who, Darin? Like Jenta? You told me the both of you met through the gym…is that what you were going to say?"

Tears stung my eyes and I didn't really know where all the emotion was coming from.

Yes, you do, the thought suddenly came to my mind. *You do know.*

I did. Every single day when it came to Jen, I found myself wondering about her mother and if I were doing things for her child and with her child the way that she would have been doing it.

Whether or not Darin said it or not, I had the feeling he compared me in the same way. It was like the unspoken phrase in the room whenever I tried to make a decision about Jen or did something for her: Would Jenta have done that? Would Jenta be okay with that?

She was gone, but I swore it was like she haunted my mind.

"That's *not* what I was going to say," his mouth said, but his eyes told me he was lying. "I wouldn't compare you to Jenta."

Frustrated, I grabbed up Jen who was pulling at my leg for attention, and held her in my arms.

"Yes, you would!" I shot back, louder than I'd initially intended. "Yes you would, because you compare me to her every day! You don't say it but you don't need to. I can feel it just by how you watch me every time I'm with her. You don't think I hear you when you're talking to her about her mommy, trying to make sure Jen knows I'm not her? Some things don't need to be said, Darin, because they can be felt!" I jabbed my finger at him as I spoke but on the way back down, Jen shifted in my arms and my elbow came down, knocking her hard and right in the eye.

"Oh shit!" I yelled as she started to scream bloody murder. Her mouth was open so wide that I could see her tonsils and straight down her throat, as huge teardrops slid down her cheeks

"I'm so sorry, Jen!" I wiped the tears on her face away to examine the spot where I'd hit her. My heart clenched in my chest when I saw it was already turning red.

"TAN! What did you do?!" Darin shouted as he walked over to me.

"I didn't mean to hit her, I just—"

Before I could finish, he snatched her out of my hands and examined her face.

"Shit!" he cursed as he looked at it and tried to calm her down. Her crying subsided a bit as her father rocked her. I watched them, silently. I felt like shit.

"You need to watch what the fuck you're doing when you're holding my damn daughter!" Darin shot at me as if I needed anything else to happen or be said to make me feel any lower than I did already.

"I didn't mean to, Darin!" I apologized. Standing up, I tried to reach out to rub Jen's back, but he snatched her away from me.

"You sure?!" he snapped. "You never wanted her here to begin with. And it seems like a coincidence, at just the moment that you were bitching about her mother that you would hit her in the fuckin' face!"

"Are you serious? You can't think that was intentional!" I squinted as I narrowed my eyes at him. "I know you must be in your feelings because there can't be any way that you can stand there and tell me that you would be in a relationship with someone who you think would abuse your daughter!"

Silence fell between us, and every single second of it, I experienced the most discomfort I'd ever felt. The last few months with Darin seemed to have changed his entire opinion of me as a person.

Or had it? I'd always been selfish, jealous, arrogant, careless, and focused on only my wants and needs, but Darin had always loved me in spite of that. That was something I knew no matter how much I'd always tried to ignore it. However, it seemed that when it came to Jen, he saw me as that same selfish bitch that I'd tried to change from ever since the day Jenta died. Obviously, Darin wasn't convinced.

"I'm sorry, Tan," he said finally. He turned to me but I couldn't make out his face through the tears in my eyes.

"You're right. I wouldn't be with you if I thought you would deliberately hurt Jen. I don't know why I said that," he continued.

But I do, I thought to myself. I knew why he'd said it and it was simple. He didn't think I'd changed.

"I'm not the person you still think I am," I told him as I wiped my tears away. "I know that I was a bitch to Jenta until the day she died… but I'm not that person anymore. I love Jen as if she were my own."

"I know," Darin admitted as he came over and planted a kiss on my forehead.

I looked down and saw that Jen was drifting off to sleep, safe, secure and comfortable in her father's arms.

"I'm going to go lie her down," he said with a sigh as he wandered away down the hall.

Nodding my head, I wiped the last traces of my tears away and sat down on the couch, hoping that all the fights were in the past and there to stay. I'd fought enough when it came to Mello…although it was physical fighting, it was mentally grueling just the same. I couldn't take any more fighting with Darin. I just wanted to be happy and to have my family.

Chapter Six

SHANECIA

"So I have good news and I have bad news. Which one do you want to hear first?" Blitzstein started as he crooked his hooded brows over his dark brown eyes and danced his gaze back and forth between my face and Legend's.

"Don't bullshit with me, Blitz. What's the news?" Legend told him, clearly agitated already.

Glancing at him, I raised one brow and wondered if I should offer him one of the pills that I was still using to treat my anxiety. I'd stopped for a bit but after they'd gotten locked up the night of Maliah's wedding, I started back. This time, I was hiding it from Legend. I knew from before that if he knew I was still using, he would make me stop. And I couldn't. This was the only way I was able to get through the days and be strong.

Everybody expected me to always be there for them. Shit, I expected to always be there for everyone. Too many people depended on me for me to have to deal with my own fears of Legend being taken away from me. He was looking at spending the rest of his life in a jail cell...there was no way I could vent to him about the little shit that crossed my mind each day. I had to be strong for him.

"Well, the evidence that they were able to obtain in order to get an arrest warrant was deemed illegal because it was illegally obtained. They had an illegal tap on Quentin's phone and heard him telling Quan about how he told you all where to find Mello and how you all finished him. He didn't mention the FBI agent but being that she was killed the same time as Mello...it was easily deduced," Blitzstein informed us, as he pushed his thin glasses further up on his nose. "I must say, he did try to be cryptic with the information but his meaning was easy enough to pick up on."

Blitzstein was the youngest attorney I'd ever seen who was as good as he was at what he did, or maybe he just looked that way. He couldn't have been a day over 30, but yet he had the demeanor and confidence of an attorney who'd been practicing law for as long as he'd been alive. He was also very handsome and had an impeccable style. I assumed that Legend and his brothers paid him very well for always having them covered.

"Rookie move to say some shit like that over the phone. How do we know that Quentin didn't know his calls were being listened to?" Legend queried with one brow lifted and his handsome face pulled into a tight frown.

I watched as he lifted one hand up and wound it around his wrist. A gesture that I'd noticed he'd been doing a lot more lately. It was almost like he was trying to calm himself down. This shit was stressing him out just as bad as it was doing to me. I needed to go back to Spelman and, more than anything, I wanted to escape the craziness around me. But, I knew I couldn't. Things were different now. I'd pledged my life to him and I couldn't leave Legend when he needed me most.

"After listening to the call, I'm very doubtful that Quentin knew he was being listened to. He admitted to being involved which made him just as guilty as the three of you. If you haven't heard from him, it may be because he was arrested too. I could check on that, if you would like me to—"

"Naw," Legend cut him off quickly. "I don't give a shit about Quentin, B. You know that. So I'm free. What's the bad news?"

Sitting down on the arm of the chair I was in, Legend leaned back and folded his arms in front of his chest as he waited for Blitzstein to continue. Looking up, I felt my heart began to throb in my chest as I waited as well. I'd had enough bad news for the rest of my life. I didn't want to have to deal with anymore.

"The bad news is that they know for a fact that you three had something to do with the agent's death. They just can't prove it. They will be on your asses every single day of your life. Even if you move to Atlanta, your brothers will still have to deal with the FBI watching their every move, in order to catch them for something small and throw everything they can at them."

Blitzstein sighed and shook his head. He took his glasses off of his face, making himself seem casual, as his face broke from his regular professional and stoic expression. Turning to Legend, he gave him a look that seemed more like one that would come from a friend rather than an attorney.

"You gotta leave this street shit alone, L. I've been helping y'all cover your asses for a long time, but I can't protect you from this. I got you out this time but next time they'll be smarter about it. You gotta stay out the streets."

Legend jumped up so quickly that he almost made the chair fall back…with my ass still in it. I had to flap my arms around to maintain the balance but he wasn't even paying attention. Blitzstein had told him the last words he'd wanted to hear.

"What do you mean, B? The streets are how I earned my living! How the fuck do you expect me to drop everything just because them pigs trying to case a nigga up?" Legend shot back at him with a question that was impossible to answer.

In the midst of Legend's rage, Blitzstein did something that few could do. He stayed perfectly still and composed without a shred of fear in his eyes. As I watched him with curiosity, I realized that they must have some history outside of Blitzstein only being Legend's attorney.

"You expect me to legitimize my illegal shit like you do, huh? Become a businessman in public and do my dirty shit in private?"

My eyes widened once Legend said that, and Blitzstein took a quick glance at me before fixating back on Legend.

"That's exactly what I expect you to do. You don't have a choice," Blitzstein said as he placed his glasses back on his face, once again returning to his professional demeanor that I now saw he wore like a costume.

He was the present day Clark Kent. Able to change his entire appearance from street thug to attorney using only a pair of glasses.

As he placed them on his face, the sleeve of his suit fell down slightly, revealing part of a tattoo that cut off just around his wrist.

"Don't act like this is something new, Legend. This is why I work so hard to clean the money you make. After the last scare, we knew that you needed to make an exit plan. You've got one…you need to use it."

With that, Blitzstein grabbed up his briefcase and did an about face to leave, locking and closing the door behind himself as Legend stood silently, processing what he'd said.

"Bae…you gotta listen to what he's saying. I don't want—"

"You don't want what, Neesy? You don't want me to work no more? You want me to sit on my ass and not do shit all day? That's the type of nigga you want to be with?" he roared at me, his sudden and unexpected anger bringing tears to my eyes. But I wasn't about to back down. I was prepared to fight for us this time, even if he didn't want me to. Jumping up, I gritted my teeth and looked him square in the eyes before starting to speak.

"No…but you have money invested in other areas. So it's not like you wouldn't be able to support us. The only thing that is bothering you is having to give up all the power that comes with being 'Legend'. I don't give a fuck about that and neither will anybody else if you're locked up for life!"

Legend's eyes were wide as he looked at me and I could tell that he was shocked at the fact that I was ready to go toe-to-toe with him about this. And I was.

"Baby, listen for a minute," Legend began again, his shoulders slightly slumped and his voice a lot softer than it had been earlier. "I'm not like you…this is all I've ever done with my life. My brothers and I had to work hard for everything that we've earned, and this is how we've done it. I don't know how to be some 'sit up in the house' kinda nigga. And I definitely ain't getting no desk job or no shit like that. I don't know what to do if I'm not in the streets…it's where I feel most comfortable. Except for when I'm up in-between them legs but you ain't been givin' a nigga no ass so…shit, what the fuck you want me to do?"

Pursing my lips, I rolled my eyes at him. Leave it to Legend to bring up the fact that I'd been holding out on him into a serious conversation.

"Honestly, that's probably why my ass is stressing the way I am. If you hit me off with a lil' something every now and then, I might be able to think straight and find a way out of this bullshit I'm in," he suggested with a straight face.

"Really, Legend?" I scoffed, crossing my arms in front of my chest. "So not getting any is the reason for all of your problems?"

He shot me a sideways smile and then licked his lips in a way that made something start to stir inside of me. My eyelids felt heavy as my body began to ooze with lust. Clearing my throat, I shook it off but it wasn't fast enough. Legend had caught the entire thing.

"It may not be the reason for my problems, but getting some of your juicy stuff will damn sure help me deal with this shit," he joked as he walked up close to me. "Stop playing and acting like you don't want this dick."

Before I could walk away, Legend pushed forward, laying his hardness right on top of my mound. I grabbed onto the chair beside me to steady myself and keep from falling.

"Stoooooop, Legend," I said gently, fully aware that I was on the losing end of this battle. "You know I want us to be celibate until we get married. They say it'll bring us closer..."

Before I could finish the rest of my thought, Legend reached down and picked me up. My legs automatically opened for him, betraying my quickly fading will, and straddled his waist, pushing his hardness right up against the place he wanted it to be. The only thing separating us was the thin material of my panties since my dress was lassoed around my waist.

"No, what you mean is you want to *celebrate* not be celibate. You want us to celebrate the fact that you will be my wife soon and I'll be pushing up in this pussy for life."

Carrying me to the room, he licked my ear and I felt myself begin to push my hips even more into him. Fuck being celibate and all the great things that it was supposed to bring. There was no way we could get closer than we were anyways. Every part of me belonged to Legend, but I still wanted to wait to make our wedding night special. And as soon as we were married, I was going to show him what it meant for me to be his forever...over and over again until he'd had enough.

Chapter Seven

LEGEND

The one thing about always being up to no good is that you stayed paranoid at all times. There wasn't a day that I was swerving through the streets in my whip that I wasn't also watching my surroundings to see if I was being trailed. And that's why only after a few minutes of driving, I noticed a car trailing me. Never one to avoid a confrontation, I pulled over, grabbed my pistol from where it sat pressed against my spine, and jumped out of my ride.

To my surprise, the car behind me pulled over to the side as well. As soon as I saw who it was behind the front window, I placed my gun back into my stash spot behind my back and crossed my arms in front of my chest, as Agent Martinez stepped outside of her car.

"You ain't got better shit to do than to watch me?" I queried as I glared at her.

Her eyes shined as if she was holding back a laugh as she walked towards me. That was one thing I didn't like about her ass. She didn't know when to take shit seriously. One thing I wasn't doing was playing with her ass.

"The fuck you grinnin' for?" I asked, finally getting sick of the smug look on her face. "I been giving you a lot of passes on this disrespectful shit on the strength that you the Feds, so you need to get the fuck out my face and do your fuckin' job."

"Or what?" she shot back, her tone coarse and her eyes narrowed as she stared at me. "Or you'll kill me like you did Agent Honduras?"

Gritting my teeth, I squeezed my fists together at my side and tried to calm myself down before I lost it.

"I didn't have anything to do with that bitch's murder. And stop fuckin' followin' me. Where I'm goin' ain't safe for pigs."

With that, I turned around and headed back to my car, unable to stand in front of her and have decent conversation with my gun so close. In those brief moments of being there, I'd already thought of pulling it out and ending her ass more than a few times, by shooting her in multiple places. The thought was becoming too real to me and it was getting too hard for me to stop myself from wanting to do it, so I had to leave. But what I did know was that there was a way to get to her. I just had to figure out what it was.

Everybody had a breaking point. With ambitious men, it was usually pussy, money and power. With ambitious women, it wasn't always that clear but I would figure it out.

"Don't go too far. And I'll be watching you," she said, further pissing me the fuck off.

"Agent Honduras must have been yo' bitch, judging from the way you all over a nigga," I gritted just as I got to the car.

"What? No..."

The sound of her voice made me look up and I saw that her smug expression had broken and been replaced by a new bewildered expression that amused me. So she was definitely not gay judging by how she was obviously put off by my comment.

Without saying another word, I stepped into the whip and drove off, leaving her standing behind me with her arms folded in front of her chest and that same dumb look on her face. As I glanced out the rearview mirror and looked at her expression, I couldn't help but laugh. She'd gotten under my skin a few times before but, this time, I'd won.

*****

"Yo' lady here?" I asked Quan once he'd answered the door.

He shook his head.

"Naw, I had a feelin' you was comin' so I sent her and the girls home." He backed away from the door and waved me in. "C'mon in, bro."

Keeping a straight face, I walked in and sat down on the couch, leaning forward as I tried to get my mind ready to interrogate Quan like he wasn't the same brother that I knew. My heart told me he didn't have shit to do with us getting locked up, and I trusted my instincts. But my gut was telling me that he was still trying to protect that shady ass twin of his.

"You want a drink or something, Legend? I got Henny, Crown—"

"Where the fuck is your bitch ass brother?" I asked, cutting in and going straight to the reason for my visit.

"Second thought, fuck the drinks," Quan muttered as he walked over to the living room and sat down across from me.

Sighing, he ran his hand over the top of his head and shook his head before steadying his gaze on my face.

"I haven't seen him. I spoke to him," he clarified when he saw the doubt in my face. "But I haven't seen him because regardless of what bond we have as brothers, he knows that I'd fuck his ass up if he had anything to do with y'all gettin' locked up."

"Okay, but why didn't his stupid ass get locked up along with us? We takin' all this heat for shit that he did. He's the one who murked that bitch!"

I wasn't believing for a minute that Quentin didn't have shit to do with what happened to us for the simple fact that he was the only one there who hadn't got picked up. If the Feds knew enough to not get Quan because they knew he wasn't there, then they should have known enough to know that Quentin was.

"Quentin did get picked up," Quan countered with a blow that I wasn't expecting.

"What?"

"I had to post his bail," he continued, lifting up a red cup to his lips before taking a sip. "He got locked up the same time y'all did, he just said that he couldn't be in the same place because he feared for his life. I posted his bail and was told that he got out a little after y'all did."

"Hell naw," I said, standing up. Running my finger over my low-cut beard, I let my mind think over everything that Quan was saying. If it was true that Quentin was locked up too, I know Martinez had questioned him and, obviously, he hadn't snitched or she wouldn't still be trailing my ass.

"To be honest, I wasn't expecting that shit," I admitted.

Quan stood up and walked over to me. "For real, I think there is a lot that we don't know about Quentin, but what we do know is that he's not trying to be against us. That nigga is fucked up but he don't have nobody but us."

"I don't give a fuck who he has or doesn't have," I told Quan, shaking my head stubbornly. "He ain't got no place here."

Quan pushed his lips together in a thin line, obviously disappointed that I was once again reminding him that I was stuck on the fact that I didn't want shit to do with Quentin. As far as him being in my life…I wasn't interested in it. There was no need. I didn't have shit that I needed from him. And on top of that, I couldn't do that to Cush. Regardless of him being forced or not, he still fucked her head up and she went through a lot of shit because of what he did. I couldn't ignore that. My loyalty was to her. Fuck that nigga forever.

"If you hear from him again, let me know," I instructed Quan as I walked to the door. "And you can tell him I'll be looking for his ass. I know Martinez told him not to leave the city. If he was stupid enough to listen to her, which I'm positive he is, then he's still here and I'll find him."

Quan didn't respond but I didn't expect him to, and that was okay. He heard me and I knew he wouldn't betray me, even if it came to Quentin. He might have thought that nigga was innocent but I didn't, and that was all that mattered.

When I returned to the house, I could smell Shanecia burning something in the kitchen and, despite my bad mood, it put a smile on my face. That was the thing about having a good woman to come home to; she made everything right just by being there. I never wanted her to leave me but I knew she had to go back to school. I promised that I wouldn't hold her back and I was a man of my word. Even if circumstances had changed, my word didn't, and I had to stick to it.

"What the hell you burning up in here?" I asked as I walked into the kitchen.

Shanecia was standing over the stove with a distressed look on her face. Her apron was covered with some kind of red stains that I guessed was tomato sauce. Her hair was all over the top of her head, going in about three different directions, and her face was spotted with sweat. My baby was putting in work...over spaghetti. Who the hell looks like this over cooking some damn spaghetti? Shanecia couldn't cook for shit!

"It's spaghetti. I was reading over some chapters for an essay that I hadn't even started that's due tomorrow, and I burned the sauce," she admitted as she pulled the pot off the hot eye and placed it in the middle to cool. "Baby, I'm sorry. I was trying to have something ready for you to eat when you got back since you haven't really been eating."

Laughing, I turned her around and picked her up, placing her on the countertop.

"I got all I can eat right here," I teased as my hands went to the band of her shorts.

Batting me away, she shook her head. "I can't...remember we said that—"

"I didn't say shit! You did!"

I stepped away, annoyed. I was stressed to the max and here she was with the perfect remedy, but she had the shit on lock because of some bogus garbage she'd read somewhere.

"Toss that shit, I ain't eatin' it," I told her, turning my nose up at the spaghetti. "I know what I want and yo' ass holdin' it hostage. How the fuck a nigga decide to make someone his wife and then she decide to put the pussy on lockdown?"

I looked at Shanecia but she didn't say a word, only glared at me. I could tell that I was pissing her off but I didn't give a fuck. She was pissing me off too!

"Matter of fact, give me back that damn ring!" I yelled, holding my hand out.

Frowning, she gazed at me for a minute as if to gauge if I were being serious. I wasn't but I was being a child because she was treating me like one. She shifted and I watched as she prepared to pull the ring off.

"Don't fuckin' try it!" I shouted, even louder. "I better not ever see that fuckin' ring off your finger, you hear me?"

Crinkling up her nose, Shanecia frowned at me and nodded her head. She was confused as hell but shit, that's what happens when you put a nigga under severe stress. I had to deal with everything that was going on around me and then come home and be on pussy punishment. This shit was fucked up.

Turning around, I walked down the hall and to our bedroom. Or my bedroom because if Shanecia was going to continue acting like she wasn't my chick, she was going to be sleeping in the guestroom from now on.

"Matter of fact…" I started as a thought came to my mind.

Grabbing up her favorite body pillow from the bed, I marched right down to the guestroom and threw it on top of the bed. Then I fucked up the sheets just to spite her because she always complained about how she liked beds to be made before she laid in them since she was able to sleep better. I didn't understand that shit, but her ass wouldn't be getting good sleep tonight. By the time I left out of there, half of the comforter was off the bed and that was what her ass got for being so damn stingy.

I stormed back to our room, huffing like a child but feeling better about what I'd done to the bed I would be making Shanecia sleep in. But when I walked inside, what I saw was definitely not what I was expecting.

"Damn…" I moaned in a deep tone as my eyes fell upon Shanecia who was lying on top of the bed butt-naked with her legs closed and her knees pointed in the air.

Then, as if she could turn me on any more, she parted her knees and gave me a view of Candyland.

"I'm sorry, baby," she apologized with a sexy pout on her face. "You were right, it was a stupid idea…You have enough going on and I don't want to add to it."

Dropping my clothes, all of my worries and every bit of my fucked up day at the foot of the bed, I dove in, headfirst, right between her thighs. She tasted even better than she looked. It was an impossible feat but like her man, Shanecia was able to do the impossible.

Lifting up, I watched the way her chest rose and fell as she panted erotically and looked at me in a way that told me she would never want no other nigga but me. She gave me life with a single touch from her hand. But it was amazing what being inside her could do.

"Oh God…" she gasped as I pushed into her, feeling her softness envelope me in her love.

"Shit," I cursed as I plunged inside.

While I was locked up, the thought had crossed my mind so many times about how I wouldn't be able to feel this type of connection with her if they didn't let me go. Being inside of her enabled me to experience the most honest and untainted love. She was the purest love. She loved me in a way that no one ever had; without judgment of my flaws or blind admiration of my strengths. She didn't worship me because of my name. She was real and so was her heart. It was unyielding, untamable and unmerited.

I didn't deserve her and never would. I just hoped that God kept shedding His grace on me so that she would never know that.

"Got dammit, Neesy!" I gritted through my teeth when she locked her legs around me and pulled me deeper into her soft folds.

I told her ass about trying to control shit but she just didn't listen. But this time, it was feeling too good for me to stop.

"Fuck!" I cursed as I spilled my seed right into her, giving her everything that I had.

Her body shuddered as she had an orgasm of her own, and I

watched her eyes roll to the top of her eyelids. She was dizzy and drunk in our love. As much as she tried to play, it was obvious she missed my ass just as much as I'd missed her.

"Damn," she whispered as she rolled over and closed her eyes.

Laying down next to her, I cradled her from behind and wrapped my arm over her chest as she drifted off to sleep. I closed my eyes and listened to the thump of her beating heart, noticing that it matched the pace of mine as I fell, for the first time in forever, into a peaceful sleep.

Chapter Eight

MALIAH

"Ohhh SHIT!" I cursed through clenched teeth. I was trying to be quiet but Murk was fucking the sense out of my ass, and I couldn't think about anything but what he was doing to me.

Still uneasy about having sex while I was pregnant, he was dicking me down carefully, but that shit was doing my lil' girl downstairs just right and I felt myself creaming for him even more so than I did ever before. I was face down, ass up, and he was kneeling behind me with his hands full of my big, fat ass, holding the cheeks apart as he eased in and out slowly.

"Fuck, Li…this shit feels so good. Ain't nothing like pregnant pussy. Shit!"

His words turned me on even more and I wanted to throw it back on him hard, but the way he was holding me stopped me from moving. The only thing I could do was grip the sheets and take his dick, just like he liked it.

"You want more?" he asked me, suddenly speeding up the tempo a bit.

Ain't a bitch in history who could salivate for dick as much as I was right then. And that's how it always was with us. Regardless of how much we had sex, which was a lot, every time with Murk was like my first time. And it had gotten even more intense since he became my husband. Every time he hit it right, I knew for sure that his body was all mine and it just did something to me.

He sent me through the kind of highs that I never knew were possible. It was a science to it and he was the only one who understood my body in that way. For the first time, I could understand what it meant to be dickmatized. I was just lucky that Murk was my husband because he had what it took to make a bitch walk around with mismatched clothes and shit, with her hair all over her head, crying and hollering for a man who ain't worth shit just so she could get another hit of his dick. It was addictive and I was a junkie for him.

Shit…I can understand why Alicia's crazy ass used to do any damn thing for a hit, I thought to myself as Murk continued to plunge into me.

"Stop teasing me, Murk! The babies will be fine!" I told him as I tried to squiggle out of his grip some so that I could throw it back on him. He had sped up but he wasn't putting his full length inside of me. I was tired of him acting like I was so damn fragile all the time.

"Let me do this, ma," he told me, slapping my hands away, and I rolled my eyes while blowing out hot air. He was so damn stubborn. This was not my first damn time being pregnant…as he so often reminded me.

"But—"

Before I could say anything, he lifted up one of my legs straight back, making me have to balance on one knee and my elbows that were firmly planted on the bed.

"FUCK!" I cursed as he started long-stroking me from the back. With my leg in the air, it made it so he was pushing inside of me but also sliding directly against my clit. When he pushed his thumb into my ass, I went insane and came instantly.

Less than a minute later, Murk was spilling his seeds inside of me by the bucket, or at least that's what it felt like. If I wasn't already pregnant, I definitely would have been then.

"I'm about to take a shower. I have some business to handle later," he mumbled once we were done, before looking at his watch.

Waving my hand at him, I turned and laid all the way down on the bed, tucking a pillow under my head. I already knew that Murk was going to head out because that's what he did. He always made sure to have sex with me before he left. Sometimes I wondered if he did that in order to keep himself from being tempted by other women, but I tried to brush that thought away.

"Alright, I'll get in when you get out," I told him.

Without replying back, he stepped into the bathroom and turned on the shower. As soon as the water began to run, his cellphone went off from beside the bed. I squeezed the pillow tighter under my head, determined to catch a cat nap before the girls came home. But then it chimed again and curiosity got the best of me. I wanted to know who the hell it was blowing up his damn phone.

When I saw the name on the screen, I instantly saw red. Like Legend, Murk also saved numbers under nicknames instead of real names. Whoever was texting him was under the name 'Good Pussy' and I was about to send myself into early labor if I didn't calm the hell down.

Grabbing the phone, I unlocked it with ease. Murk didn't know that I'd discovered his passcode. He never really tried to hide it when he entered it into his phone, so I figured he didn't have anything to hide inside of it. That's why I'd never used it until now. In less than a second, I was opening up the text message, eager to see what it said but, before I could read it, the bathroom door opened.

I gasped and pushed the phone up underneath the covers as quickly as I could. When I looked up, Murk was standing in the doorway of the bathroom looking right at me with a blank, unreadable expression on his face. I felt my own face getting hot and I knew my cheeks were red. My heart was slamming in my chest, the way it did when you knew you had no business going through your man's phone but did anyway. I couldn't understand why the hell I was feeling all panicked when obviously *he* was the one in the wrong.

"That's for you and me now?" Murk asked finally as he walked over towards me, his towel wrapped around his waist although he hadn't gotten in the shower yet.

"Wh—what do you mean?" I asked him casually. I rolled over on the bed and laid down, as I tried to pretend that I hadn't been up to anything and had no idea why he was so mad.

Then suddenly, two hard fingers dug deep into my shoulder.

"OW, MURK! You know I hate when you do that shit!" I yelled, swatting his hand away and rubbing on my shoulder. "I bruise easily. Shit!"

"Give me my fuckin' phone, Li," he told me but he tossed the covers back and grabbed it up himself. "The hell you goin' through my shit for anyways? What the fuck I do in the streets don't concern you. Don't need you signing your own death certificate by thinking you can run away on a nigga or some shit. You won't have it good like your wimpy ass cousin did. I'm not Legend…I'll come find dat ass."

Smiling, he licked his lips and cut his hazel eyes at me, but that gesture didn't get the response from me that it normally would have. While rolling my eyes, I sat up on the bed and glared at him.

"Don't try to play cute with me, Murk. Who is 'Good Pussy' and why is she texting your phone?"

The smile instantly fell away from Murk's face and was replaced by the pokerfaced expression I'd gotten used to seeing. It was like a defense mechanism and I'd begun to hate it. Whenever Murk wanted to close me off so that I couldn't read him, he would retreat back to the survival mechanisms he'd developed from growing up in the streets, the blank unreadable expression he'd perfected being his most successful tactic.

"Don't do that shit. Don't try to cut me off. Tell me the truth," I told him as I stood up from the bed and looked directly at him.

"Tell you the truth about what?" he asked. "She's just some chick I used to know. I didn't even know I had her fuckin' number still in my phone."

There was more to the story and I knew it from the way that he spoke to me so easily and so rehearsed. His words were void of emotion and his expressionless face was still intact, telling me that he was still trying to block me from something. He was operating with too much control. The way someone did when they had something to hide.

I knew that there was no way that Murk was cheating on me because he didn't have it in him. He didn't have the patience for that shit, and he was too much of an asshole to be sneaking around and shit to spare someone's feelings. But whatever was up with him and whoever Good Pussy was, I was going to find out.

"Alright, baby," I told him. "Well, then it should be nothing to block her number, right? Since you're married now, you shouldn't have no more use for her."

Nodding his head, he picked up his phone and pressed a few buttons, making sure that the screen was turned so I could see.

"There you go, Li. She's blocked," he said once he was finished. "No need for you to be sneaking around in my shit."

"Yeah, yeah, yeah…" I rolled my eyes and then waved him off as he started to walk back towards the bathroom. "Hey, can you get me some food from Pollo Tropical before you start work?"

Murk whipped around and looked at me with his eyes wide.

"Hell naw, you get that shit! You need to walk there too. I'm hiding all the damn keys. All you been doing is sitting around here, eating and getting fat," he shot back at me, using his normal rude and abrasive humor.

"Murk, how can you say that?! I'm pregnant with your big head babies! That's why I'm so hungry all the damn time. This is *your* fault!" I was fuming mad at him. How dare he call me fat?

"No, that's *your* fault. I ain't never gotten a chick pregnant. But you only been with two niggas in your life and your ass done got pregnant by the both of us. You can't help but get pregnant, but you can help the fact that you overfeeding my jits and then sitting around here getting all big and pale and shit. Go out and get some sunlight. Yo' yella ass look like a fuckin' ghost."

I sucked my teeth loudly as Murk walked in the bathroom and slammed the door behind him. I couldn't take him seriously at all. He was so damn rude all the damn time that if I was the kind of chick that wore my heart on my sleeve, I'd always be in my feelings.

Standing up, I pulled on my robe and went to take a shower in the other bathroom so I could get dressed, get DeJarion together and leave. Since he wanted to act like an asshole, I was going to do exactly what he said and get some fresh air with my baby.

*****

"Do you believe him? I hate his ass, Neesy!" I scoffed as I spoke to my cousin on the phone.

I was walking down the street with DeJarion in his stroller. After only being out for about 15 minutes, I was starting to see that this was a terrible idea. Not only was I sweating bullets, but my clothes were drenched from sweat as well. The only good thing was that the heat had knocked DeJarion out, so he was no longer hollering and carrying on how he had been when we'd left.

"Li-Li, you know that Murk is rude as hell so I don't know why you always acting surprised by that shit," she reasoned with a giggle at my expense.

"Well, if a tan is what he wanted me to get, that's what's gone happen. It's hot as hell outside," I told her as I looked off into the distance and wiped sweat off my brow.

"Who you telling? I'm already chocolate but I swear I got a few shades darker from when we were waiting for them to be released. How are my twin babies?" she asked, changing the subject. Her voice rose up with excitement and made me wonder if she was catching a whiff of some baby fever.

"They are good…making me eat up every damn thing I see and can't see. The way I'm putting on weight is crazy though. It's definitely not like with my other pregnancies. Murk is right…I been getting fat as hell."

"Li-Li, you ain't never been skinny…you always been thick and that's one of the things Murk loved about you. Don't let him fuck with your mind with his bad sense of humor. And you're not getting fat… you're having two damn babies!" she reasoned with me again, and I could almost see her rolling her eyes at Murk on the other side of the phone.

But she was right.

"Well, enough of that. What's up with you and Legend? Everything going okay with your plan of being celibate?" I asked her with a malicious smile on my face.

Being celibate before getting married was my idea, and I told her to do it while knowing there was no way in hell that Legend would go for it. I tried it on Murk and it lasted for about 28 good hours, but when I finally gave in, he tore my ass up like he'd been in prison for 10 years.

"Hell naw, Legend wasn't going for that shit. The only reason he lasted as long as he did anyways was because when I got him home, his ass passed out in the bed and didn't wake up until morning. After Blitzstein left earlier, he was on my ass and hasn't let up since."

"You're welcome," I told her, doing a horrible job at stifling my giggles. "I knew that shit wasn't going to last long."

"What?! Heffa, you the one told me about that article you read!"

She sounded genuinely upset and that only tickled me even more. Shanecia was so damn predictable. You could get her to do anything as long as you told her you read about it in a book.

"I ain't read no damn article. I listened to Steve Harvey and got the idea. The only reason I told you it was from an article is because I knew that's what your educated ass needed to hear in order to do it."

I laughed so hard I had to stop walking. People were staring at me as I stood on the sidewalk all by myself, laughing my ass off, but I didn't care. Hell, messing with Shanecia was funny.

"That's so mean, Li. I really was going to try to do it too!"

"Girl, don't knock Steve Harvey. He knows what he's talking about. And besides, from how he explained it, I'm sure it's in a book somewhere—"

I was cut off by the loud sound of a car approaching at top speed from behind. My mouth dropped open and I whirled around, noticing that it seemed to be incredibly close to me.

Not only was it close, it was damn close. I instinctively closed my eyes and grabbed the stroller closer to me as the car continued to speed to where I was. It wasn't until the driver spun around, doing an illegal U-turn in the middle of the road and stopped, with the passenger side facing me, that I saw who it was.

"MURK! YOU FUCKIN' SCARED THE SHIT OUT OF ME!" I yelled with the phone still pressed against me face. "Neesy, let me call you back!"

"Maliah, get yo' round ass in the gotdamn car! What muthafuckin' time you on right now?!" Murk yelled out of the window.

Two seconds later, he'd jumped out of the car and was storming over to me with his eyes pulled into tiny slits. It had been a long time since I'd seen him this upset.

"What is your problem?" I asked as he scooped DeJarion up, put him in my arms and then started to fold up the stroller.

"The fuck you mean, what is my problem? I was in the damn car waiting for your ass to finish getting ready so I could drive you to the fuckin' store to get your greedy ass something to eat. After waiting all damn day, I decide to walk in the house and remind your ass that I got shit to do just to see that you already left! The fuck?!"

Glaring at him, I walked to the running car to put DeJarion inside, and closed the door before turning my vicious gaze back onto him.

"You *told* me to walk to get something to eat. You *said* I was getting fat!"

"All this muthafuckin' time and you still ain't able to see through my bullshit?!" He paused and I just blinked at him like he'd lost his damn mind.

Nobody could see through Murk's bullshit. He was completely unreadable when he wanted to be. How the hell could he expect me to tell the difference?

"You're my wife now, Li! What the fuck kinda nigga would I be if I had my pregnant wife flat-footing it 'round the fuckin' city so she could get something to eat? Does that even sound like me?" he asked as he poked his finger into his chest. "I'm the same nigga who won't even give you all the dick because I'm scared it'll hurt you. Does that shit really sound like me?!"

"He said the dick hurt! Whew, JESUS!" I heard a woman gasp somewhere in the background, making me instantly aware of the fact that we were arguing right in the middle of the sidewalk.

"I'm sorry, baby," I told him as I dropped my head.

He was right. I was so used to messing with Danny's ass, who never had a problem with me walking anywhere for shit. I needed to forget the past and realize what kind of man I had. I was married to a real nigga.

"Get in the car, Li," Murk said, his voice lightening in tone as he ran his arm around my waist and ushered me to the car. "Don't do this shit again. Realize the kind of man you got."

Nodding my head, I stepped into the car and took a deep breath. He was absolutely right.

TANECIA

Sighing, I flipped through the classifieds as Jen laid in her bassinet holding a half-empty bottle to her mouth. She drank it down like I'd starved her all day. One thing that she did more than anything else was eat and it showed. She was one chunky baby but I loved it.

"You look like you could go for some more. Huh, Juicy Mama?" I asked, using the nickname I'd given her. She giggled up at me, proudly showing off her gummy mouth.

"So pretty," I cooed as I looked down at her. "Now if you could only help Tee-Tee figure out what she wants to do with her life, we'd be all good!"

Reaching down, I released her from the harness and allowed her to crawl around freely so that she could play with her toys on the floor. Then I went back to the most torturous thing I had planned to do for the day: look for a job. I was still undecided on whether I wanted to work or go back to school. Noting that I wasn't the best student, I decided to look for a job first and, if that fell through, then I would go back to school.

After searching for about five more minutes and finding nothing that would pay over minimum wage, I decided to stop what I was doing for the time being and give my sister a call. Shanecia was younger than I was, but she was the voice of reason in the family and it had always been that way. She rarely did things without thinking them through and she tried to act through using her reasoning skills, whereas I ran purely on emotion.

"Hey, Tan!" Shanecia greeted me in an extremely chipper way that I wasn't quite prepared for.

She seemed all tore up about having to leave Legend with the mess he was dealing with, the last time I'd spoke to her.

"Hey, bish," I replied back and she gasped.

"TAN! Where is Jen?"

"She's right here," I replied, looking over at Jen who was sticking each of her building blocks in her mouth as if the different colors had a different taste. "She don't understand what I'm saying, Neesy. Chill out."

"Okay, let her start going around and calling people 'bish' and I'll see what happens."

"I'll pop her on her ass. That's what will happen!" I responded as if she should have already known it. And she should have. Wasn't too long ago that I had to pull our own mama off her ass. Shanecia knew all about a good ass-whooping.

"Anyways, I called because I need some help. I was thinking about going back to school and—"

"TAN! That's so gooood! I'm so proud of you for—"

"Neesy, calm down!" I interrupted her with a frown. "I'm not finished yet! Anyways, I was thinking of going but we both know that school was never my thing, so I asked Darin if I could work at the gym and he said—"

"Gym? As in g-y-m?" she cut in.

"Well, yes. Bitch, what other gym you know of?" I snapped and she started laughing. Even though she'd pissed me off, I started laughing, too.

"Uh!" I warned Jen when I saw her about to stick one of my shoes into her mouth. Reaching out with my foot, I moved it out of her way when she dropped it and continued my conversation with Shanecia.

"Anyways, I'm just lost and I don't know what to do but…Jen, I said no!"

Once again, Jen had my shoe in her hand and was about to pluck it right between her chubby jaws. Reaching out, I leaned over and grabbed the shoe from her again and tossed it. Then I popped her on her hand.

"I said no! Do not put that shoe in your mouth, it's dirty!"

Reprimanding her hurt me more than it did Jen because my heart tore into pieces when she poked her bottom lip out and started to cry.

"Awww, you popped the baby," Shanecia's soft ass said through the phone, making me feel even more terrible for popping her.

I was about to reply but I felt the heat of someone's stare on me so I paused. When I looked up, I noticed it was Darin staring at me from the entrance of the hall. He'd been in the room watching something on TV but from the look in his eyes, he'd been standing there watching me long enough to be upset about something.

"Neesy, let me call you back," I told her and hung up before she could answer because I knew Darin was about to get in my ass for some stupid reason.

"Why would you hit her?" he asked as he walked into the room with an accusatory gleam in his eyes.

"Because she kept trying to stick my shoe in her mouth even though I told her no!"

"She's a baby!" Darin argued. "That's what they do! She doesn't know what you're saying when you tell her no!"

"Well, she does now," I muttered under my breath. "That's the point of popping young kids. They understand when they do something wrong, they are told 'no' and get popped! You pair the word with the punishment and they begin to understand what 'no' means!"

With a stubborn scowl on his face, Darin folded his arms and glared at me.

"My mother never hit me," he informed me. "She used other ways…more positive ways to discourage my negative behavior, and I think I turned out just right."

He gave me a condescending look as if to suggest I hadn't, and I wanted to wring his neck.

"Fine," I replied. "Your daughter. Your rules."

Darin turned to walk away but I had another thing for his ass. He wasn't about to use me like that.

"You need to take her with you to the room," I spoke to his back. "I think she'll experience a more 'positive' environment in there with you while you watch the game."

Frowning at me, Darin walked over and grabbed Jen in his arms without saying a word, and then disappeared down the hall. As soon as he was gone, I took in a deep breath and let it out slowly before picking up my laptop to search for more jobs and fill out more applications. I had to figure out a way to find a job so I could get the hell out of Darin's house.

*****

"HEY, BABY!" Darin's mother, Diane, exclaimed as soon as she walked through the door.

My bad day was about to turn straight to shit, and I knew it as soon as I heard that she was coming. I was still convinced that Darin had her come over just to spite me because he knew I hated his mama. She was one of them women who did all kinds of low-down shit in her past, but forgot that her past wasn't clean as soon as she made it out of the hood. With Darin's successful business, she was sitting pretty in a small condo right off of South Beach. She claimed it was her retirement home, but her ass had never worked a real job a day in her life. She was a hustler in her youth and ran the streets with Darin's father, but you wouldn't know it from how she acted. And because of her newfound bourgeois nature, she felt compelled to constantly remind the both of us that I wasn't good enough for her son.

"Oh, you still here," she said as she walked in the room with her eyes narrowed at me as she cradled Jen in her arms. Jen was reaching up for her hair and I prayed that she would snatch Diane's wig clear off.

"Yes, I am," I replied smugly before turning back to my laptop.

"Unfortunately," she sneered and I took a deep breath, trying to hold my tongue. "And what's this about you thinkin' you can put your hands on people's children?"

I cut my eyes at Darin who gave me a look that told me I was on my own. He had snitched to his mama for a reason, and he wasn't interested in saving me from her disrespectful ass.

"You know what? I don't have to take this shit," I muttered, snapping my laptop closed.

"Tan—" Darin started.

"Naw, you're good. Stay here and soak up the air with your mama," I said, holding my hand up to stop him from coming near me. "I'm out."

This time he didn't even try to stop me as I walked right by him and grabbed the keys off the table. They were his keys, but I dared him to say something about it. Thankfully, he didn't, because Diane might have had to pull me off her son.

About 15 minutes later, I was pulling up to my destination: the rehabilitation home that my mama was in. It was funny how life sometimes made you reconnect with people you had long ago written off. Lord knows I had made up my mind about Alicia a while ago and swore I wanted nothing to do with her, but since she'd been in rehab, I'd been visiting her and found out that she understood me more than anyone else.

She knew what it felt like to want to rebuild yourself in the midst of people who didn't trust that you really wanted that. She knew what it felt like to be surrounded by people waiting for you to turn back into who you used to be.

Unfortunately, as my relationship with her grew, the one she had with Shanecia turned to shit. Shanecia didn't seem to really want anything to do with our mama. She would ask about her to make sure she was completing her treatment, but she wouldn't visit her and rarely called. It wasn't like Shanecia to act that way, but I figured she just needed her time.

"Hi, Tanecia! How are you today?" the quirky, blond receptionist, Taylor, greeted me once I walked into the building.

"I'm okay," I said although I didn't feel it. "How's my mama?"

"She great! I'm so proud of the progress she's made!" Taylor admitted with a genuine smile.

"Me too." I thought back to how one day I'd been there and Alicia threw a cup of pudding right at Taylor's face. She always seemed to give Taylor the hardest time in the beginning. In fact, it took a while before she would even call her 'Taylor' instead of 'white bitch' or 'pink toes'. Mama had come a long way.

"There is someone else back there but he comes all the time and never stays long," Taylor told me, piquing my interest.

Instead of asking her who it was, I started walking down the hall to my mama's room, wondering who the 'he' was that was visiting her. I prayed to God that she hadn't found someone to bring her drugs in here.

When I got to her room, I peered inside from around the corner to see if I could catch whoever it was that was in there with her. When I saw who it was, I relaxed instantly and shook my head. Legend.

"Listen, Boogie…you better not be tryin' no shit," he was saying to her. "We need you to get better. The doctor says you been doing good but you know I know how a fiend moves so you can't trick me.

I'mma fuck yo' ass up if you don't do what you need to do to get out of here."

Gasping, I put my hand to my mouth and tried not to laugh out loud. I already knew Legend was disrespectful as hell and sometimes that shit rubbed me the wrong way, but this was just plain funny.

"A'ight, Legend. I hear you," Mama replied back drily. I could almost hear her rolling her eyes through her words.

"Don't hear me. You better feel that shit because I ain't playin'. I want to marry Shanecia but I need you to be right because she'll regret walking down the aisle without you there."

"I promise. I don't want this shit no more, I'm good. Tell my daughter I said 'hi', okay?" she asked him.

I walked closer and looked inside at the two of them. Mama had a hurt look on her face as she requested Legend to speak to Shanecia for her. Shanecia had always been her favorite. It was something I knew and just accepted. I was never jealous of my sister for it. I knew that she was our mama's favorite but it wasn't like she wanted it to be that way.

"I'll tell her," Legend promised. He leaned down and gave mama a hug before turning around to walk out of the room.

As soon as he turned into the hall, he ran right into me.

"What's up, Tanecia?" he asked with a tight, straight face, using my whole name.

Thank God that he had Shanecia because, otherwise, his ass would never relax. When she wasn't around him, he was all business and couldn't shed the hard exterior. I watched as he stood in front of me looking like a member of the armed forces. Shanecia brought out the soft side of him. With her gone, he was a soldier.

"Not much," I replied. "How are you holdin' up without Neesy?"

The mere mention of her name made his hard countenance break. His expression softened and a smile teased his lips before he shrugged.

"I don't know how I'mma make it without her," he admitted honestly, showing a vulnerable side that I knew he wasn't used to revealing.

"You'll be fine. She's only going to school…not to war."

He stared deeply into my eyes as he processed my words, making me feel uncomfortable by how intense his gaze was. I could see why Shanecia was in love with him. He wasn't the most emotional man, but when it came to her, he wore his heart on his sleeve.

"Not war, huh? Then why does it feel like she might not come back?" he asked, and I had to stop my mouth from dropping.

I knew Legend was in love and I knew what he felt for my sister was unnatural, but to hear him speak with such helplessness and to seem so exposed was so strange to me. I wanted that kind of love. I *had* that kind of love. But Darin had taken it away. I needed to show him how he was hurting what we were building and get the love back.

"She'll be back," I reassured him. "What you and Neesy have is real and no matter what you're going through right now, just know she loves you and she won't ever leave you again. She has that ring and she's not trying to take it off…not for anything. If you want her back, tell her she has to go to school in Miami now and I swear she will."

He thought about it for a few seconds and then shook his head.

"I can't do that to her," he said in a soft voice, as if he were talking to himself rather than to me.

Then in a flash, almost like I'd imagined the last few minutes, his face went back to normal and the Legend returned. Leith was gone... tucked inside and reserved only for Shanecia.

"Have a good one," he told me and then walked down the hall as if we hadn't been in the middle of a conversation.

Stunned, I stood there for a few minutes and listened to his footsteps thunder down the tile floor as he walked down the hall. Darin had his issues, but Legend was confusing as fuck. How Shanecia dealt with it, I didn't know, but he was the one for her. And deep down in my heart, I knew that Darin was the one for me.

"Tan, is that you?!" my mama called out all of a sudden. "I'm sober so that means I can hear good as hell. Bring ya ass, girl! I hope you got my cookies, too!"

Rolling my eyes, I laughed and walked into her room. Nothing like my mama to change up my mood.

Chapter Nine

LEGEND

"Legend, did you threaten my mama?!" Shanecia asked me as soon as her big ass head popped up on the screen.

Calling her on FaceTime had become a ritual ever since she went back to Atlanta. She had me on some sucker shit but it didn't matter. What she wanted, she got. No matter how much I tried to hold my ground with her, I couldn't. The more time went on, it was like she knew it, too.

"Hell yeah," I replied back to her with a straight face. "I told her ass that I was gone fuck her up if she didn't get better. I don't play no games with Mom Dukes. No mother of mine will be creeping up in my damn stash."

"How you gone talk to my mama like that though? Your disrespectful ass has to be stopped!" she told me with her eyes wide as if she was surprised. I was the same nigga now that I was when she met me. Why the hell was she acting like she didn't know who she was with?

"Neesy, you know ain't no nigga on the planet can stop me," I reminded her cockily. "But if it makes you feel any better…I said it to her out of love."

Shanecia rolled her eyes and popped a gummy bear in her mouth from an open bag that she had out of the view of the screen.

"Your ass always eatin'. Damn, you sure you not pregnant?"

I joked around with her about that a lot, but this time I was seriously wondering if she was. Shanecia had always been greedy so her eating didn't mean shit to me. But I would be lying if I didn't point out that her face seemed to look greasy as hell. Maybe that was the 'glow' I always heard her talking about her cousin had since she'd become pregnant.

"I'm not pregnant. Don't you think I would know if I was pregnant, Leith?"

"Chill with all that Leith shit, Neesy."

"Well, that's your name!" she reminded me with a smirk.

"Yeah, and don't wear it out," I playfully tossed back at her, pulling a line from my childhood days.

"You so damn immature sometimes," she scoffed.

She shifted a bit in front of the screen. Her top fell and suddenly I got a nice eyeful of the top of her mocha-colored breasts. My eyes lingered there for so long, I didn't even realize that she was watching me just as intensely as I was watching her.

"You like what you see?" she inquired although the answer to her question was obvious.

The sound her voice, light and teasing with a hint of seduction, let me know that the bad girl in her was about to make a strong debut.

"Hell yeah," I replied back, licking my lips.

She didn't say another word but in less than two seconds, she'd slipped her loose-fitting top down to expose her bare breasts, complete with her perfect chocolate nipples.

I didn't dream of women. I dreamed of money. But if I ever had a dream about a chick, Shanecia would be it. It was deeper than her looks and even deeper than the way that she felt when I was inside of her. It was everything she was. She was the perfect light to my dark. The remedy to my evil. God had shed some grace on a nigga when he brought her into my life, and I was indebted to him forever for being able to share any bit of my life with her.

"Shit…" I moaned when she started playing with herself, pinching her nipples and licking her lips.

The bulge in my pants was growing larger and larger with each passing second. Feeling self-conscious, I looked around my bedroom even though I knew that I was the only one in the house. Her lil' freaky ass was giving me a peep show and if she kept going, I was about to have to pull my man out and relieve some pressure.

"You want more?" she asked me with a teasing smile on her lips.

"Yes," I said, although I was shaking my head 'no'. She had my whole mind fucked up.

Shanecia giggled at how confused I was and I had to chuckle my damn self.

"You need to stop before I come find your ass," I warned her when I saw that she'd stood up and was shimmying her shorts down her slim thighs. She was trying the fuck out of me if she thought that she was gonna show me some pussy and I wasn't going to be hitting I-95.

"You can't leave, Legend. You know that," she told me, but I made a swatting motion with my hand to dismiss every single thing she said.

"Fuck that shit. You keep fuckin' around and I'll be in Atlanta by nightfall."

It was more of a promise than a warning but obviously, Shanecia wanted to call my bluff because a half of second later, I was staring at the perfectly trimmed triangle between her legs. My mouth was watering like a damn dog and my dick was beating up against my zipper, as she did a little dance in front of the screen, rocking her hips back and forth while she titillated her nipples.

"You want more?" she asked again.

"Fuck no," I replied honestly.

She giggled and she continued with her little peep show. Fucking with Shanecia was about to get my ass locked up again. After about five more seconds of watching her stick her fingers in places that I wanted to put my tongue, I'd had enough of that shit.

"Fuck it, I'm on my way," I grumbled, licking my lips.

Laughing, Shanecia stopped what she was doing and shook her head at me.

"Legend! You can't—"

Before she could even fix her mouth to finish that statement, I closed my MacBook, ending the call, and stuffed it inside the laptop bag next to where I was sitting. I didn't even need to pack clothes because I'd buy all that shit once I got to Atlanta.

Grabbing a duffle bag, I threw some knots of cash, the laptop bag and a few other items I needed inside of the bag, and draped it over my shoulder before checking my watch. I could be at the airport in about 30 minutes and, hopefully, catch a flight that would have me in Atlanta before dark.

My phone rang and I almost ignored it, thinking it was Shanecia trying to convince me not to come but when I looked at the screen, I saw it was Murk.

"What's up, nigga?"

"Aye…man, I did some stupid shit," he started, catching my full attention. Murk usually was on top of his game so when he said he did some stupid shit, it usually meant he really did.

"What happened?" I asked him, pausing before I walked out the door.

"You remember that broad I messed with at Li's job? She in my phone under 'Good Pussy' and Li saw that shit when she texted me today out the blue. I was praying to God she didn't ask me who the fuck it was texting me."

Sighing, I shook my head. My brothers always found themselves in some shit over another female, and I was glad I didn't have them kind of problems.

"I thought you ain't fuck her…why the fuck you have her in your phone under 'Good Pussy'?" I questioned him as I started to gather the last of my things together out the house.

"I didn't save her fuckin' number under that stupid shit... *she* did because she thought it was gone make me keep dealin' with her ass. I forgot I had her number in my phone!" Murk replied back. "But I can't explain that shit to Li...she gone swear I fucked that bitch."

"Yes, she will," I cosigned. "Don't tell her shit. Delete the bitch's number and just do whatever stupid shit Li wants you to do, like coming home early and all that other gay ass shit...then she won't have nothin' to worry about."

Murk was quiet for a few seconds as he mulled my words over in his mind.

"That's good advice, yo. Thanks, man," he said finally.

"Don't mention it. I'll hit you up later...'bout to catch a plane to ATL."

"Oh, you goin' to see the little lady, huh? Knew your ass couldn't stay put for long without her," Murk teased, putting a smile on my face.

"Ya damn right, nigga. One," I replied before ending the call.

I walked out the house and threw the duffle bag in the back seat, before hopping in my G-Wagon and pulling out of the driveway. But as soon as I turned out of the gates in front of my house, who did I see sitting on top of her damn car, staring right at me? Agent Martinez. I was sick of this shit.

Pulling to the side, I put my car in park and jumped right out of it, walking right in her direction. She was sitting on the hood, holding some coffee drink that she was probably sipping on just to keep her ass up so she could annoy the fuck out of me.

"The fuck you want?!" I asked, keeping a safe distance as she pulled herself off of the hood of the car. The distance was for her. I didn't want to come any closer and risk busting a cap in her ass.

"What? I'm just sitting here, taking a break and enjoying my drink!" she replied, faking surprise at my anger.

"Get the fuck outta here," I scoffed. "Haven't you been watching me enough to know there ain't shit going on for you to see? You don't have nothing to do all muthafuckin' day, huh?"

Smiling, she sipped from her drink without answering my question. I could see that my anger was satisfying for her and that was the opposite of what I wanted to do. She seemed to enjoy seeing a nigga pressed so I needed to switch my style up. Walking over, I leaned against her car and decided to try a different approach.

"You know what? Since you are so into watchin' me, how about I stay right here so you can see me up close?" I asked with a smirk.

Martinez slowly came towards me with her eyes narrowed as she held the cup in her hand.

"Don't you have somewhere to go? I saw the duffle bag that you put in the back seat," she tested me. I knew she was trying to get a rise out of me but I wasn't going to give it to her. She liked to see me blow up and lose control. It got her clit hard. She was the type of woman who would do shit to a nigga just to irk his ass because she got off on being in control of his emotions. She wasn't about to do shit with me but get all of that flipped on her ass.

89

Reaching out, I grabbed the cup from her hand and took a sip from it. It tasted like shit. The kind of shit Shanecia would like but I couldn't stand. Still, I kept my face neutral and continued to sip. She watched me carefully with one of her eyebrows lifted.

"Aren't you the least bit concerned that you don't know where my mouth's been?" she asked as she watched me continue to drain her drink.

"You got a nigga?" I asked, although I already knew the answer to her question.

Her face flushed at my question and I knew I was right. She didn't have anybody at home but herself and maybe a few cats, or whatever it was that lonely chicks bought to keep them company.

"What is this shit?" I asked, finally as I pulled the cup away and stared at it. "It's fuckin' terrible."

She began to laugh a little before answering. "Iced Caramel Macchiato…extra shot of espresso and whipped cream."

"You couldn't just order a regular ass drink, huh? Uptight ass got them in there making you some shit regular people can't even pronounce."

"It's not that bad," she shrugged, letting her guard down a little further. Biting back a smirk, I cut my eyes at her. I had her right where I wanted her.

"You're right," I told her. "I'll probably grab one on my way to the airport."

The mention of the airport knocked the sense right back into

Martinez. Her back straightened up and the frown returned to her face. But it didn't do shit to me. I'd tried her and now I was pretty much sure of what her weak spot was. She was lonely. She'd spent her career making niggas respect her at the job and locking others up...she'd pushed herself into a corner and the only person there was herself.

"Airport? I told you not to leave the city!" she reminded me as I walked away towards my car, but not before stopping to push the cup of 'iced whatever-whatever' back into her hands.

"I know what you said and I know what I'm about to do," I informed her in an icy tone, and shot her the same smug smile she always reserved for her run-ins with me. "You can't make me do shit. Stay the fuck outta my way from now on and we won't have no problems."

And with that, I chucked her the deuces, jumped in my whip, and tore off down the road. She couldn't stop me and she knew it. Her scare tactics didn't work on me but I had a tactic that would work on her. I just needed to figure out if I was going to use it.

Chapter Ten

MALIAH

"Mama, where do you go when you leave here in the middle of the night?" I asked, sitting down in the living room next to where she sat watching her soap operas.

Instead of answering my question, she cut her eyes at me as if telling me to be quiet so she could watch her show. I had half a mind to turn the TV off, but I didn't want to have to fight for my life. My mama had been in the church for a long time, but she still could pack a mean punch and I wasn't for it. She didn't care that I was pregnant; if I got in between her and *General Hospital*, it would be WWE in this bitch.

"Okay, it's a commercial now, so I'mma pause to remind you that you need to stay out of grown folks' business," she told me through her teeth like I was five-years-old again.

"Mama, I *am* grown," I reminded her, rolling my eyes.

Turning, she frowned at me with her head tilted sideways.

"Good, then you should have something else to worry about than what I'm up to! I don't need you clockin' the miles on my shit," she replied.

"Mama! You can't say that!" I gasped and shook my head at her. "You supposed to be in the church!"

"If God ain't want us to say 'shit', He wouldn't have made the word. Now, hush!" she admonished, returning her eyes to the TV. Her stories were on again so that was the end of the conversation. I wasn't going to get a thing from her now.

The doorbell rang, followed by a loud knock on the door and I stood up to answer it, taking my time as I scooted by her, deliberately blocking her view of the TV. She reached out and popped me on my ass, hard enough for me to yelp out in pain.

"Don't think you too grown to get your ass whipped, Maliah! I didn't raise you to be disrespectful," she scolded me.

"Heffa, you barely raised me at all," I said, making sure that my voice was too low for her to hear it.

When I got to the door, I looked through the peephole before opening it. Although I tried my best to stay out of what Murk was into, I wasn't stupid and I knew I had to watch my back at all times. The last thing I wanted was to end up like Shanecia's ass: tied up and drugged in the back seat of some crazy nigga's car.

When I saw that it was a white man in street clothes on the other side, I became suspicious immediately about his reason for standing in front of my door.

"Who is it?" I asked, frowning as I watched him shift his weight from foot-to-foot while waiting for me to open up.

"Paul! I live down the way and I just had a question," he said, smiling into the peephole and showing me a mouth full of coffee-stained teeth.

Rolling my eyes, I pulled away from the door and unlocked it.

"Nosey ass white peo—"

"Hi, are you Maliah Michelle Calhoun?" he asked as soon as I opened the door, throwing me off completely.

"It's Dumas now but…how do you know my name?"

Smiling, he pulled out an envelope that he had behind his back and handed it to me. Without thinking, I took it and stared with a frown on my face.

"Here you go. You've been served," he finished as I continued to gawk at the envelope in my hands. "Sorry, I had to lie!"

And with that, he turned around and ran to his car as I stood there dumbfounded and praying that what I thought wasn't in the envelope wasn't really there.

"Oh God," I muttered as I pulled out the contents of the envelope and read the first page. I must have read it over a dozen times.

"What is it, Maliah?! Whatever it is, get over it and get in the damn house! You standing there with the door open wide, lettin' all that damn light in! It's makin' a glare on the TV. I can't see shit!"

"Mama…" I started but couldn't even finish the sentence as I closed the door.

My heart was hurting. When I woke up that morning, I had the funniest feeling that something didn't seem right. I figured it was just the shit that Murk was dealing with getting to me. But now I saw that my feelings had been correct and it didn't have anything to do with Murk.

"Mama," I repeated, standing in front of her.

"MALIAH, if you don't get your big ass belly out of the way so I can watch my stories, I'mma kick your ass! And you know my knees weak so don't make me have to do it!" she yelled out with her eyes narrowed, but it didn't sway me at all.

As soon as she looked up and saw the expression on my face, I saw hers soften. She knew I needed her help. It was obvious something was wrong.

"Danny is suing me for custody of the kids—"

"CUSTODY?! How he gone do that? He don't have nowhere to stay! What can he possibly have over you to get the kids?" she asked, shooting out question after question before I could even fix my mouth to answer her.

"I don't know but he is tryin," I said with a sigh. "Why can't he just leave me alone and do his own thing?"

"Because those are his children, Maliah," she answered with a sad tone.

My mouth dropped open as I fixated my eyes on her.

"You're taking his side now?"

Shaking her head, she sighed and then shrugged at me.

"I'm not taking his side. But in a world filled with men who don't give a damn about their kids, you have to applaud him for fighting to see his. Now, I don't agree with him trying to get custody when he ain't got a pot to piss in, but that's just my lil' fancy opinion," she ended with another shrug.

My mama did have a point. One thing about Danny that I could always count on was his love for his children. Just thinking about some of the good times that we had when it was just the five of us still puts a smile on my face. Back before everything went south with us, it was like he lived for me and his kids.

Those were some of the best moments of my life…moments I'd never get back. And as much as I'd wished back then that he could get it straight and get his life together, he didn't, and I couldn't be mad about that because that's how I was able to meet Murk.

"You're right," I finally said aloud, although the words still felt like they stung my lips as they passed through. "But what am I goin' to do about Murk? He's not going to go for that."

"It's not his decision to make!" she snapped.

I cut my eyes at her and she was able to easily understand the unspoken words coming through them. It didn't matter if something was Murk's decision to make or not. If he felt a certain way about anything concerning me or the kids, he would let his opinion be known and there was nothing anyone could say about it.

"If he loves you and the children, he'll act accordingly," she said as she pursed her lips and ducked her head at me. "And if he doesn't, the judge will make sure he starts to."

That's the last fuckin' thing I want, I thought as I folded the letter back up into the envelope and walked to the kitchen to hide it somewhere Murk wouldn't find it.

On second thought…let me not hide this in the kitchen, I thought, thinking back to how he'd found my main hiding spot.

I didn't want to be dragged in court for this. I didn't want to be forced into making a decision when it came to my kids, but it looked like I was being given no choice.

"When you gonna talk to him?" my mama asked as soon as I walked back into the living room.

Frowning, I curled my lip at her.

"Don't you have your stories to watch?"

"Hell no!" she replied with a little of a dry laugh following. "What we got going on here is better than anything they can cook up! Just make sure when you tell him, I'm around to watch because I know his ass is gonna cut up!"

No he won't because I'm not going to tell him, I thought. *There is no way Danny is going to beat me in court so I'll do this on my own.*

"And don't be thinkin' you can handle this on your own without tellin' him, Maliah Michelle!" my mama said as if reading my mind. "I don't know how many times you gone try to hide something from that man before you realize he got a radar up your ass. Just tell him and get it over with so I can watch."

Grumbling under my breath, I walked away from her and down the hall to text Shanecia and ask her to give me a call when she could. I knew she was probably somewhere laying right up under Legend's ass, but I needed my cousin to tell me what I should do.

Chapter Eleven

SHANECIA

"Let me count the ways I love your big headed ass..." Legend started, pinching me on my nose when I frowned at him.

"Why you always gotta talk about my head, Legend?!" I huffed and pushed him away.

He laughed at me and I rolled my eyes but couldn't help joining in on the laughter. It was a lazy Friday. I'd skipped class to lay in the bed with the man who would one day be my husband. When? I didn't know. But every day that went by made me wonder what we were waiting for.

Neither one of us had large families and it wasn't like money was an option, so we could get married at any point. But Legend hadn't mentioned the wedding since I agreed to marry him and I was beginning to wonder why.

"I always talk 'bout your head because it's big as hell," he explained with a shrug as if everyone should've known the answer to that. "I hope our kids don't inherit that five-head of yours."

Laughing, I pelted him with a pillow in the head. He ducked out of the way but I still caught him right in the nose.

"Oh, now you wanna mention children?" I smirked as I eyed him. "I thought you were against them."

"I am against them," Legend explained. "And, matter of fact, we definitely ain't havin' none."

He slid his hands behind my backside and cupped my ass, pulling me closer to him.

"But you know...ain't nothin' wrong with practicing."

I leaned over and planted a kiss on his lips, soft at first, but then he squeezed hard on my ass and I went in deeper. This was what love was supposed to feel like. If we could have this moment forever, my life would be complete. Unfortunately, I knew that life would happen and I would have to let him leave. This was the part of a long distance relationship that I hated to the core. We operated on borrowed time.

Right now, I was in Legend's arms but in a couple days he'd be gone and I'd be on my own once again. Now that we were getting married, it was harder for me to stand being without him. I hoped every day the legal issues he was facing would go away, and he wouldn't have to worry about his brothers being watched so we could go along with our lives and enjoy each other.

Legend's phone rang and I felt the shift between us when I lost his attention. Business was calling. Sighing, I pulled away and watched as he shot me a lopsided smile, showing off his perfect dimples and chiseled jawline. His facial hair was unusually unkempt but with everything he was going through, I wasn't surprised. He was under a lot of stress and I wasn't around as much as he probably wanted me to be in order to help him relieve it.

"Yo," Legend answered the phone, putting it on speaker.

Lifting one brow, I watched him curiously. This was obviously a call he wanted me to hear because any calls dealing with his business in the streets, he always took in private.

"Legend, I'm almost positive that your brother, Quentin, has something to do with the case the Feds are tryin' to bring against you," Blitzstein said from the other line.

With wide eyes, I looked up at Legend and watched as he closed his eyes, clenched his jaw tight and then let out a long protracted sigh. Right then, I realized something that no one else did, including Legend himself. No matter how he acted and what he said, in his heart of hearts, he wanted Quentin to be right. He didn't want to be against his own flesh and blood and it didn't sit right with him. At the same time, he knew that he couldn't lay down and let Quentin ride with doing the disrespectful and traitorous shit he was doing. He would have to do something about it and I knew, deep down, it hurt him to have to.

"How do you know that?" he asked through his teeth when he finally opened his eyes.

His tone was tight and his face was blank, but I knew his mind was racing with various thoughts and emotions. I could tell from the way that he continued to bite down on his back teeth and wind one hand around the wrist of the other. Everyone had a way of showing when they weren't at ease and I'd long ago found his.

"I went to meet with Agent Martinez and afterwards, I was in my car about to leave when I saw him walk up. At first I thought it was

Quan but Quentin has a certain…air about him that makes it obvious that he's the evil twin," Blitzstein explained and I shook my head. How Quentin could turn on his own brothers when he had no one else in the world was beyond me.

"Well, he's gonna be the fuckin' dead twin when I find that nigga," Legend gritted, grasping the phone hard in his hand as he sat up.

I let my eyes glide down the front of his bare chest and watched the subtle way it rose and fell as he took in quickened short breaths. No matter how cool his face appeared to be, it was obvious he was furious and hurt by what was going on with his brother.

"I trust you'll let justice be served," Blitzstein commented in a way that made me feel as if he was unofficially cosigning Legend's threat on Quentin's life.

They continued to speak as Blitzstein went onto another subject about Legend investing in some business opportunities, but I zoned out of the conversation when my phone chimed. Leaning over the opposite side of the bed, I grabbed it off the nightstand and checked the screen. It was a text message from Maliah.

Can you talk?

I looked over at Legend and saw that he'd taken the phone off speaker and was deeply engrossed in the conversation.

Yes. I'll call you now, I wrote back.

Grabbing my robe, I wrapped it around my body and tiptoed out of the room, cradling the phone in my hand. When I walked past Legend, he reached out and tapped me lightly on the ass right before I slipped out of the door.

"What's up?" I asked Maliah when I got to the living room.

"Danny is suing me for full custody of the kids! I just got the subpoena today," she blurted out so fast I could barely focus on the words she was saying.

"Uh…what?!"

"What nothing, Neesy! This nigga has lost his muthafuckin' mind!"

From Maliah's tone, she was close to crying but I could see why. She was pregnant and dealing with a lot of stressful situations coming back-to-back.

"You know Murk is not goin' to be cool with this shit. What should I do?" she asked and I shook my head before I replied. I couldn't believe she would ask me that. She must have forgotten who she married.

"Li-Li, you need to tell Murk about this today," I told her with sincerity. "You can't hide this from him because he will find out and it may be worse when he does."

"But don't you think I can handle this on my own and—"

"No. Tell him what's goin' on. You married him so you can't hide shit like this from him."

As soon as I finished talking, I heard Legend call me from the room. Before I could reply back, I saw him pop out from the hallway looking sexy as hell, with a huge bulge poking out the front of his sweatpants. Smirking, he bit down on his bottom lip and grabbed it as he eyed me. It was time to go.

"But what if he—"

"Maliah, I told you what you should do!" I interrupted her, most of my attention on Legend who was now licking his lips as he gripped the large print in his hand. "Now I gotta go, but you better do what I said or you'll be in some deep shit. Bye!"

Without waiting for her to reply, I hung up the call and tossed the phone down on the sofa, turning off the ringer so we wouldn't be interrupted. After that, I followed Legend back to the room with a smile on my face.

We'd been making love to each other all morning already and from the looks of it, Legend wasn't anywhere close to being tired. But neither was I. If I wasn't pregnant already, by the time he left Atlanta, I definitely would be.

LEGEND

Spending time with Shanecia was just the kind of therapy a nigga needed. But now it was time to head back home to take care of business. Although my brothers were more than capable of dealing with shit, until I was able to get rid of Agent Martinez for good, I knew that they couldn't really make the moves that they needed to.

Murk had already told me that he'd caught her posting up around some spots on the block that we usually conducted business so he had to shut down on some transactions that we needed. One thing for sure…I was tired of her ass.

She was bad for business. I had to find a way to get rid of her and quick, but I couldn't do shit while I was in Atlanta with Shanecia. I couldn't focus on anything but her when she was around. All we'd done since the day I showed up was fuck and then turn around and make love. I was hungry as hell because we barely ate. The only reason I was giving her a break now was because she had work to do and Cush had come over.

"So when y'all gone make some babies or something?" Cush asked me as she flipped through a magazine, her eyes planted on the pages. "I could use a little one running around to take my mind off the fact that I'm not doing anything with my life…"

"When you goin' back to school?" I inquired, changing to something I was more comfortable discussing.

Cush lifted one brow and glanced at me with a sly smirk on her face, letting me know that she knew full well what I was trying to do by changing the subject.

"Legend, you asked Neesy to marry you but you don't want to talk about having kids? You know that's ass backwards, right? And you do know with Murk and her cousin having two on the way, it won't be long before she starts gettin' baby fever, right?"

Cush winked at me but I just stared back at her. I wasn't feeling this shit she was talking at all. With a sigh, Cush rolled her eyes and decided to continue with the subject change.

"I'm going to go back now that it's safe," she started, her eyes looking off into the distance as if she were thinking. "Now that I know Quentin wasn't the one who had crept into my place and Mello is dead, I guess there isn't anything stopping me from going back. I took a leave, so I'm good to go once I get back in NYC."

"Blitz sayin' that Quentin was the one who ratted us out," I told Cush, not fully sure why I mentioned it.

Then again, I did know why. I knew that I was going to have to go after Quentin and I knew that also meant I would have to go head-to-head with Quan. Cush was a good medium between me and Murk because, although she had the hot temper and somewhat violent nature, she was able to level it out by reasoning a little better than we did. Murk and I were the "shoot first, ask questions later" type, while Cush was more analytical and wasn't known to make knee-jerk decisions.

"I don't think I believe that, Legend," she said, shocking the hell out of me. "I probably should be the last one to speak on Quentin's behalf..."

Pausing, she chuckled nervously for a bit as I watched her with narrowed eyes, wondering what it was she was about to say.

"...but at the same time, when he spoke to you at your house that one time and explained everything...I believed what he was saying. I could tell he was telling the truth. He doesn't want to be against us. He did a lot of fucked up things but I know that he was telling the truth... Gene made him do it. And he still chose wrong but he didn't think he had any other choice...and I forgive him. I can't tell him that to his face yet but...I forgive him."

By the time she'd finished speaking, there were tears streaming down Cush's face. Reaching out, I wiped one as her words echoed through my mind.

I forgive him.

I felt a weight lift off of me. I hadn't realized how much pressure I'd felt for not being able to help Cush deal with the emotional turmoil that came from Quentin's actions. Just hearing her say that she forgave him and watching her let all that hurt go, through her tears, changed something in me. It had affected me deeply that Cush was experiencing that sick shit right across the hall from where I'd slept when we were younger and I couldn't do anything to stop it. That weight had stuck with me for the rest of my life.

"I'm happy now...and I know myself," she continued as she wiped more tears from her face. "I don't think Quentin had anything to do with the charges brought against you, Dame and Murk. If Blitz didn't hear Quentin snitching, then you can't just accept what he says as truth."

"That's why I love you, sis," I smiled as I reached out and hugged her, kissing her lightly on the forehead. "I gotta head back to MIA in the morning and Neesy's gonna be at the library for a minute. You wanna watch a movie or some cheesy shit y'all females be wantin' a real nigga to do?"

Cush laughed and rolled her eyes before punching me in the arm, but she still nodded her head.

"Yeah, let's order something to watch until Neesy gets back because I know, once she gets here, both of y'all asses will be holed up in that room."

"Damn right," I replied with ease before cracking a smile.

Cush laughed again and grabbed the remote so we could find a movie to watch. I stared at the screen as she flipped through movies and made comments to me about what each one was about, but my mind was still on what she'd said.

Was it possible that Quentin was innocent? And if he was…could I forgive him?

Chapter Twelve

QUENTIN

I sat drumming my fingers against the table, feeling anxious as hell about sitting in a room with a federal agent, the same one who was stalking my brothers, right across from me.

"Are you going to speak, Quentin?" she asked me, trying for the third time to get me to say something to her ass.

Wasn't happening. They could call me a lot of things but I ain't never been no snitch. Well…not when it came to my brothers anyways.

"Quentin, you do realize that if you know anything and you don't tell us, we could have your prior deal revoked. We could send you back to prison."

Punching my hand onto the table, I jumped up.

"Don't fuckin' lie to me, bitch! You can't do shit! I did my part and I got the signed papers to prove the deal we made, so don't try that shit! You asked me to give up some of Mello's men and I did that shit! I told you what you wanted to know and y'all muthafuckas let me out of prison. But if you think I'mma tell on my fuckin' blood then you just as stupid as you look, you crazy ass bitch!"

From the way Agent Martinez's lips twitched at the ends, I could tell I was getting under her skin and that's exactly what I'd wanted to do. Just because I took medication to keep my mind right didn't mean that I was dumb. I knew my rights so she was gonna have to come harder than she had.

"We can place you at the scene of the crime—"

"You can't place me at the scene of shit! That's why y'all muthafuckas had to let me go. You heard something I said on the phone…something you obtained through *illegal* means and that's all yo' stupid ass got! If you had somethin' else, I would be in a fuckin' cell! You gone have to come harder, love."

Sitting back down, I crossed my arms in front of my chest and gave her a smug look; the same one that she'd worn on her face when she watched me walk up in this bitch, thinking she was gonna be able to make me snitch on my fam. They say once a snitch, always a snitch… and, hell, it wasn't a full lie. If I could get my ass out of some shit by tellin' on some muthafuckas I didn't care about, I would. But I drew the line at tellin' on my brothers. I'd fucked up my fam enough already.

"You were out for less than a month and not only were you seen with your brothers, who we told you not to contact, but a federal agent has been murdered and so has the man who issued a reward for your death when you were released from prison. We already have enough to charge you for something just off that!"

"Then do it," I urged her with a malicious tone.

Jutting my chin out at her, I clenched my teeth and glared at her.

If she thought she was going to get me to say shit, she had lost her damn mind. When I saw the look in her eyes shift, exposing her inner-thoughts of disappointment, I knew she'd finally gotten the picture.

"Get the fuck out of my face," she ordered, sitting back in her chair with a scowl on her face. Martinez was pissed off but I didn't care. I'd won. I wasn't the weak link that she'd thought I was. I couldn't turn on my blood.

*****

"Thank you, bro," I told Quan as I walked inside of his apartment.

He held the door open, welcoming me inside, but the look on his face showed me that he wasn't the least bit thrilled about me being there.

"Don't mention it," he mumbled, following me to the living room.

I chuckled a little but he lifted his hand up.

"No, muthafucka, I'm serious! Don't fuckin' mention this shit! Legend already been over here askin' if I seen you," he informed me as he sat down and sighed. A stress line formed in his forehead.

"What you told him?" I asked, a little bit of an edge to my voice.

I really loved my brothers. All of them. I loved Cush, too, but I wasn't brave enough to tell her that. I'd fucked up whatever relationship Cush and I could ever have, and the best thing for me to do was to stay out of her life. But I really wanted to make things right with Legend, Murk and Dame. Quan was my twin and he'd always be on my side as long as he knew I wasn't doing no crazy shit, but I still needed to win over the others.

"I told him I hadn't seen you but you know Legend ain't believe that shit. You hungry?" he asked me and I nodded my head. "Okay, I'll get you somethin' to eat but you gotta get the fuck up outta here."

"Where I'mma go?"

Quan thought on it for a minute before answering.

"I have a little spot I used to take chicks at so I didn't have to bring them here. Since I'm in a relationship or whatever…you can use it."

"Thank you, man," I said with a smile. I still didn't know what the fuck I was gonna do with my life, but at least I had a spot to lay my head.

"Don't mention it," he repeated, giving me a look to make sure I knew that, once again, he meant it in the literal sense. I nodded my head.

"Do you think he'll ever come around?" I asked, thinking back to Legend as Quan started pulling food out of the fridge.

"Who, Legend?" he inquired and I nodded my head before standing up to walk over to where he was.

"Um…yeah. Legend is a stubborn nigga but he has a heart, thanks to Neesy, anyways. He's been doing some shit I didn't think he'd ever do…he's calmed down a little so he'll come around, just give him time," Quan said with a shrug. "The one you gotta worry about is Murk."

"Murk?" I repeated, lifting one eyebrow. "But if Legend is cool with shit, I figured Murk would forgive me, too."

Pressing his lips together, Quan shook his head sadly.

"That's where you wrong, bro," he continued. "Legend is the leader of the two, but Murk has his own mind. He respects Legend enough to follow his decisions but, in actuality, he's the more dangerous of the both of them because he always has Legend's back. To have someone's back…that means you're slow to trust and slow to forgive, even if they do. If Legend forgives you, Murk won't…he'll always be on the sidelines waiting for you to fuck up so he can shoot you in your shit. And he may never come around. You can forget about warming up to that nigga."

Quan laughed a little and shook his head before throwing some food on the stove as I sat and thought about what he'd said. I understood what he was saying and although I had been gone a long time, I knew when it came to Murk, he was right.

"And Dame?"

Quan started to laugh. "Now you and me both know that nigga is softer than a rabbit's tail. He's street-raised but it's not in his heart. He's too much of a romantic for that shit. If Cush forgives you, then he will, too. Same as Legend."

Smiling, I nodded my head and decided to be at peace with what I could get, even if Murk never came around. All I wanted was another chance at having some type of family. There was nothing like being able to know you belonged somewhere. Even a street nigga like me desired that.

Chapter Thirteen

MALIAH

"**M**aliah, you're a fuckin' coward for this shit," I muttered to myself as I tried to get dressed so I could leave in time for the custody hearing.

Even though Shanecia and my mama had told me to tell Murk about the subpoena, I still hadn't gotten around to it. It wasn't that I didn't want him to know, it was that I didn't want his ass to invite himself to the hearing. Not only would it be a bad idea to have him and Danny in the same room, anyone with two eyes could tell that Murk was pure thug, and I didn't want the judge to take in his icy, cold demeanor and that's when she made a judgment on the case.

"Where you goin'?" a voice said from the door and I nearly jumped 10 feet in the air, knocking my big toe on the leg of the bed in the process.

"SHIT!" I cursed as it throbbed. But that pain was the least of my worries.

Whipping around, I looked at the entrance of the bedroom and saw Murk standing there, in all of his gangster glory, shooting stone cold glares in my direction as he leaned against the door pane.

"I said, where are you goin'?" he repeated coolly.

His eyes slowly traveled from my face down to my clothes: a simple black pantsuit with a white shirt underneath. In my hand was one of the black heels that I planned on wearing; I had been searching for the other when he startled me.

"I—uh, I'm goin' to—I mean..."

"Don't lie, Maliah," he warned, using my whole name.

His hazel eyes narrowed and I flinched under his stare. It was like he could see right through me. My shoulders dropped in defeat and I averted my gaze. It was over. I couldn't lie to him even if I tried. He knew me too well.

"When were you goin' to tell me about the subpoena?" he asked and I didn't even feel compelled to ask him how he knew about it.

One thing that I should have learned a long time about Murk was that he just *knew* things. He had his ways and whatever they were, they were damn good. I couldn't hide shit from him and it was time for me to stop trying.

"I wasn't going to tell you," I admitted, tears coming to my eyes. "It's not that I didn't want you to know...I just didn't want you to come. Danny will be there and—"

"I don't give a fuck about that nigga!" Murk spat, twisting his lip up in disgust as he spoke.

"Yeah, but...I didn't want the judge to act some kind of way because of your tats and…" my voice trailed off as I tried to think about how to tell him that, for once in our lives, I felt ashamed of his appearance and wanted him to be different. At least for the hearing.

Murk stared back at me. Even without saying something, I could see that he picked up on what I'd felt, although I hadn't really spoken the words. Without saying a thing, he turned around and walked down the hall to one of the guestrooms.

"Don't go anywhere until I come out of here," he said, before he closed the door behind him.

I was sitting at the dining room table, twiddling my thumbs, when Murk finally emerged from the guestroom. When I heard him coming up behind me, I swirled around towards him and my mouth almost dropped open.

"Oh, you thought that I was only one type of nigga, huh?" he asked with a smirk on his face but I didn't give him the satisfaction of replying.

Murk was dressed in some nice black dress slacks, black dress shoes and a long-sleeved collared shirt and tie. Although you could still see some of the tattoos on his neck peeking out of the top of his shirt, to say he was fine didn't do him any justice at all. Murk was sexy as fuck and if I didn't have anywhere to be, I'd be on top of him trying to make two more babies pop up beside the buns we already had in the oven. He was *clean* to the max.

"You ready or you need a napkin for that drool on your bottom lip?" he asked, running his finger along my lip, making it flip. Snatching away, I pushed him a bit and then rolled my eyes.

"Yes, I'm ready," I said in the midst of his laughter. "Let's go."

*****

My stomach was in knots as we walked into the courtroom, and it wasn't because I would see Danny again. It was because Murk would see Danny again and the last thing I wanted was drama. But judging by all of the uniformed policemen holding their weapons in holsters at their sides, I doubted the two of them would act up too much.

"Murk…" I started right before we walked into the courtroom where my case with Danny was being handled.

He lifted his hand to stop me and shook his head.

"I'm good. Don't worry."

I wanted to believe him but I couldn't bring myself to do so. There had never been a time since I'd been with Murk that he had ever exhibited the least bit of self-control when it came to anything. Having to control his temper with Danny only a few feet away, was going to be a task.

I walked into the courtroom and my eyes immediately roamed the room for Danny's presence. I saw a few people standing around and some sitting on the benches, but none of them looked like him. Feeling some sense of relief that his reunion with Murk wouldn't happen just then, I exhaled deeply, happy for a few more minutes of peace.

Then I felt Murk's body tense up beside me and I knew that he was there. Lifting my head, I searched the room once again and that's when I saw Danny. I'd missed him the first time because he looked nothing like the Danny I'd known the past few years. Like Murk, he'd cleaned up for court and was wearing a nice black suit with dress shoes and a tie. His hair was cut and, although he was still thin, he had gained a little weight and looked healthy.

My mouth parted slightly as I stared at him, completely in awe of the turnaround he'd made in such a short time. He had a ways to go, but he almost looked like himself again.

Just as I was about to turn away from him, Danny turned towards me and we locked eyes. For a second, I saw the surprise in his eyes that quickly changed to adoration when he saw me. Then his attention went to my bulging belly and I saw the hurt. Lastly, his focus rose up and settled on Murk…that's when I saw the hate.

But when I glanced at Murk, I didn't see hate in his gaze at all. Instead, I saw a smug look plastered all across his face as he smirked and then dipped his head in Danny's direction, letting him know that he'd won the war. Then, as if Danny needed to be humiliated further, Murk pulled up my left hand and pointed at the ring on my finger. I snatched my hand away and frowned at him, but his point had already been proven to Danny. I was pregnant and there was a wedding band on my finger. In Murk's mind, there was no need to fight. The battle had been won and I was his.

When we sat down, I jabbed Murk in the side and frowned at him.

"Why you so damn rude all the time? You just came here to rub it in his face that I'm pregnant and married to you, huh?"

Murk laughed and then shook his head. "Hell naw, I didn't come for that. Anybody with eyes can see you're pregnant and married. I came so I could see the look on that muthafucka's face when he figured that shit out!"

"Ugh!" I scoffed and rolled my eyes at him but there was nothing I could say. Murk was a true asshole so it never surprised me when he acted like one.

Less than an hour later, I was storming out the courtroom with tears in my eyes. Danny may have lost the war when it came to me and him being together, but the judge had definitely leveled the playing field when it came to the kids. He didn't have full custody, as he'd initially requested, but she granted him joint custody, giving him full visitation every other weekend and some holidays, unless I could prove him to be unfit. I was enraged.

"I can't believe this shit!" I yelled as soon as I got outside of the courthouse. Standing on the steps, I watched, with Murk by my side, as Danny walked happily over to his car, with an extra pep in his step, and got in.

"You know I can finish that nigga up and you won't have to worry about this shit, right?" Murk asked as he ran his fingers along the perfectly straight line of his beard. "It'll be easy as fuck. One shot, clean to the—"

"No, Murk," I interrupted him quickly, shocked that he would still be entertaining the idea of killing Danny. "We'll just let this play out the way it's going to. Danny will be back using and as soon as I find out about it, I'm coming back to court to get all this shit reversed."

Grabbing my hand, Murk watched as Danny drove away, and I wondered if he was planning something else in that twisted mind of his. Then he shrugged and brought his attention on me.

"I'll let you handle it your way for now," he told me. "But if shit starts to go south—"

"I know," I interjected. "Believe me, I know."

Chapter Fourteen

LEGEND

With all the shit happening, I couldn't remember the last time my brothers and I all hung out at the rec center like we normally did. That was just it though. Life wasn't normal. The Feds and that damn Agent Martinez were stopping me from doing shit because she was always somewhere staring at a nigga. I was in an apartment that I had downtown now. I couldn't even stay at my house because she was always posted up outside the gates watching me come and go, with that stupid ass look on her face.

If I was the old me, I would have just fucked her and sent her on her way, stuck in love with a nigga who would never be hers. Unfortunately, that wasn't me anymore because I had Shanecia. So since I didn't know how else to deal with a bitch that had a chip on her shoulder because she needed to be fucked, she was still a thorn in my damn side.

The doorbell rang just as I was lacing up my sneaks and getting ready to go. For some strange reason, I got a feeling that it was Agent Martinez ready to fuck with me again. Things were going too good for me at the moment and I was back in Miami to handle some business. It seemed just like her to pop up at the exact moment she wasn't wanted.

But when I looked through the peephole, it wasn't her. I was actually surprised as hell at who I saw.

"Nigga, we friends?" I asked as I swung the door open.

Darin gave me a sideways look before barging his ass up in my spot like I'd invited him in. I must have missed myself giving him an invitation up in my shit.

"I need some advice about somethin', Legend," he said just as I closed the door behind me.

Turning around, I stared dead in his face and blinked a few times.

"So should I leave the door open or not?" I asked him. He screwed his face up at me like he didn't understand what I was saying.

"Huh?"

"You said you need some advice…so should I leave the door open for whoever it is you invited to give it to you?" I inquired further. "And why the hell is y'all meeting here?"

"Legend, I need some advice from you!"

More blank stares and blinking.

"Nigga, you got a brain tumor or some shit? What the hell can I give you advice on?" I asked him. "Wait…you lost the gym? You wanna run dope or some shit?"

Walking in the living room, I went over to the bar and started to make myself a drink as I chuckled to myself. Darin took a seat at one of the barstools and I continued on. I popped the top on a Heineken and pushed it to him.

"You know, D, I always knew that 'good boy' shit was a fuckin' act. And no muhfucka who grew up in Carol City as square as you. I told Neesy that I didn't believe that cheesy shit for one—"

"I don't wanna run no dope! I need advice about Tan," Darin said finally.

Frowning, I reached back over and grabbed the Heineken right out of his hands.

"Hell naw. Get out," I told him. "I don't do that shit."

"What you mean?" Darin asked with a frown as I pulled the barstool from under him and started pushing him towards the door. "You're engaged to her sister. If I marry Tanecia, we'll be brothers-in-law. Who else can I go to for advice about her?"

"Your neighbor," I told him as I continued ushering his ass back to the front door. "I got shit to do so you gotta go."

"You know, this some fucked up shit," he complained. "And why the hell you took the drink away?"

"Because a Heineken is a drink for real niggas. I would've gave you a Lime-a-Rita but I only have that shit when Neesy around. You can go visit Trell and have tea time and talk about bitch shit—"

Once again the doorbell rang just as I was about to grab the handle to the front door and push Darin out on the other side.

"You invited somebody else?" I asked him, looking at him sideways. With wide eyes, he shook his head.

"Nope."

Reaching behind me, I grabbed my pistol and held it to my side as I peeked out the peephole.

"What you gonna do with that?" Darin asked, a hint of anxiety in his voice.

"Get that bitch out your heart, nigga," I told him as I stared out the peephole. I couldn't see a thing. Whoever it is had left already.

"You know what?" I asked him as I started to open the door to check outside. "Maybe you and I need to hang out more often. I can't have my sis-in-law being caught with a nigga who can't bust a hot one in a nigga if need be."

Darin narrowed his eyes at me and I started to laugh at his expense. I was pissing him off but if he wanted to hang out with the D-Boys and be part of the team, he was going to have to be able to take a little childish jeering.

"What da fuck?!" I said once I got the door open. Darin came forward and looked out over my shoulder.

"Oh shit!" Darin cursed from behind me.

Suddenly, I heard the sound of an engine revving up as someone mashed hard on the gas. Looking up, I noticed a raggedy ass old school Chevy Camaro take off down the street at top speed. I ran out after it with my pistol out, ready to shoot at the tires to stop the raggedy ass car from rolling, but it pulled off way too quick.

"FUCK!"

I cursed as I watched it go off in the distance. It was long gone, but I still sat there and watched the space where it had disappeared, waiting for my reality to change. Finally, after what felt like forever, I turned around to Darin with my jaw clenched tightly, willing myself not to just start firing off shots for the hell of it. But there was one major reason why I couldn't do that. And the reason why was now in Darin's arms.

"So L...you wanna explain this?" Darin asked, handing me a piece of paper with some cursive writing on it.

I snatched the piece of paper from him and stared at it, reading it quickly. But two words stood out to me more than any: *your daughter*.

"FUCK!" I cursed again, making the small child in Darin's arms flinch.

"Let's go back in," Darin offered as he walked back inside my spot. "It looks like you might need my advice now."

"Hell naw, I don't need your advice, nigga! Because this lil' jit ain't mine!"

I eyed her with one eyebrow lifted and the little girl gazed at me with hers lifted as well, mirroring my expression. She had to be about four-years-old, no older. She had a mess of curly hair, thick black eyebrows, fat cheeks with dimples in each one, and the most piercing stare that I'd ever seen in a child so young. Yeah, she favored me a bit, but I didn't give a shit. She *wasn't* mine.

"I hate to break it to you, L, but she looks just like you," Darin commented as if I'd asked him for his damn opinion. He tried to walk back in my house again and I stopped him.

"Stop that 'L' shit, nigga. We ain't friendly. It's Legend," I corrected him. "And I don't care what the hell she looks like. She ain't mine!"

"My mama said you're my daddy!" she cried out, using an accusatory tone.

"Man, fuck your mama! She left you at a random nigga's doorsteps! And keep your mouth closed, lil' jit, you don't know me! You ain't never heard of 'stranger danger'?"

The little girl's eyes teared up and it made me feel like shit, but I still held on to my glare as I scrutinized her. She shrunk back from my gaze and started to clutch Darin's chest. Hell, he should keep her. She liked him more anyways.

"Legend, you can't do that. You can't talk to a child that way," Darin said with a look of disapproval on his face and shook his head gently from side-to-side.

"You would know it," I told him as I pushed by him and walked into the apartment. He followed behind me even though, once again, I didn't remember telling his ass to come inside.

"This seems like your kind of situation anyways. You already had a baby dumped at your doorstep. Just add this one to the pile," I said as I dumped the Hennessy and Coke mixed drink that I'd made for myself earlier. I refilled the glass to the brim with just Henny. I needed something strong as hell if I was going to be able to make it through this day.

"I didn't have a baby *dumped* at my doorstep, nigga. Her mama *died* giving birth to her!" Darin yelled, placing the little girl down on the floor. I did a double take at him as he came closer to me, his eyes narrowed as he spoke. Obviously, I'd got his lil' square ass angry because he was losing his shit.

"You need to stop being so damn selfish all the fuckin' time and grow the hell up! That is a child there…a life! Look in the fuckin' envelope, Legend! Her mama put her birth certificate, social security card and everything else you need inside of it. She's not planning on coming back! She left you with your kid and you need to figure out what the fuck you are gonna do."

Watching him intently, I didn't even know what to say. His ass had a backbone, that's for sure. He wasn't as soft as I thought. I raised the glass to my lips to take a swig of my drink but before I could, Darin snatched it out of my hands.

"And the first damn thing you need to know is you can't fuckin' get drunk around your kid!"

"Listen, nigga, I gave you a pass during your first rant but you ain't gone be yelling at me in my own fuckin' house. Secondly, I told you she ain't mine."

"Alright, well prove it," Darin countered, his voice a lot lower than it was before. His ass wasn't crazy. "But until you do, you're going to have to take care of her."

Glancing over, I saw the little girl was staring at me with a frown on her face and her hands on her little hips, firmly in Darin's 'amen corner' and cosigning every damn thing he was saying.

"Well, at least you ain't ugly," I told her.

For some reason she found that funny and started to giggle. Confused, I just watched her. She was laughing but I was serious.

"What the hell is that you got on?" I asked as I looked at the dirty ass clothes she was wearing.

Whoever her mama was, she wasn't shit. She had her in a dirty white t-shirt that was stretched across her belly and tucked into a short pink skirt. But the worst part of it all, she looked like she was still wearing a damn diaper.

"This my favorite clothes," she informed me, her little attitude still intact.

"Well, they look like they belong in my favorite garbage. Take that shit off."

She looked at me like she wanted to punch me dead in my shit and stood her ground. Hell, maybe shorty was mine.

Walking over, I grabbed up the bag that her mama had left, and the first thing I picked up was her birth certificate so I could see who her bitch ass mama was.

"Da fuck?!" I said as I looked at it. "This bitch scratched out her own damn name so I can't see who she is. Who the fuck gives somebody a birth certificate to use and got her name scratched out?"

Darin looked over my shoulder and fell out laughing. Shaking my head, I looked on the next line at the little girl's name.

"Onika Miraj Dumas," I read in disbelief. "Stupid ass mama."

I looked at the little girl and she poked her bottom lip out. "You like that name?"

She shook her head hard, her mess of curls shimmied around the crown of her head.

"Well, what name you like?" I quizzed her, crossing my arms in front of my chest.

Her eyes curled upwards to the ceiling as she thought a bit on it.

"Princess Elsa," she told me.

"Princess...Elsa?" I repeated with wide eyes. She nodded her head.

"Alright, I'll call you Princess Elsa. And *if* I'm your daddy...when we get this shit straightened out, we'll get your name legally changed to that, okay?"

Smiling, she nodded her head again and I couldn't help but smirk at how cute she was, in spite of how pissed I was at the situation.

"Legend, you can't name her—"

I put my hand up to stop Darin from telling me what the hell I couldn't do. His ass had just preached to me about what I *needed* to do and now that I'd taken his advice, he wanted to stop me. It was time for his bad luck ass to leave. He'd been here less than five minutes and somebody had dropped their shorty off at my crib. I didn't need any more of his bad karma.

"We tossing the rest of this shit that's in this bag, okay?" I told her. "Let's go get you some new clothes. We got somewhere to go."

She nodded her head again but then her face fell as if she remembered something. Running over, she grabbed the bag from my hand and pulled out the most hideous doll I'd ever seen in my life. It looked like her head had been through the fuckin' meat grinder. Most of her hair was missing and her clothes look just as dirty as Elsa's.

"Put that ugly shit in the bag!"

"NO!" she yelled back at me and clutched the doll to her chest.

"I said put it in the bag! That shit ain't welcome in my house!"

"I said NO! And you said you ain't my daddy so you can't make me!"

"She got a point there," Darin piped in as he looked over my shoulder.

"Nigga, pump yo' muthafuckin' brakes then do a U-turn and get the hell out." I absentmindedly waved him away and then focused back on Elsa.

"Listen, I'll get you a new doll. *That* doll looks like it eats babies when you sleeping. We can't take that ugly shit with us. We got a reputation to uphold."

Elsa looked at me with narrowed eyes and pressed her lips together into a straight line. She was prepared to go toe-to-toe with me even if it took all day. She wasn't budging. I needed to try a different approach.

"Listen…I got swag. It makes people be nice to me. Don't you want some?"

She frowned her face up at me like I was an alien. Ten minutes in and I was already failing at this daddy shit. I was glad this lil' jit wasn't mine. I just needed to figure out who she belonged to and get her ass out before Shanecia found out about this shit.

"Okay, you like food? You look hungry. You hungry?"

She nodded her head.

"Well, I can't give you no food as long as you got that ugly ass doll in my face. She messin' up my stomach. So go take her somewhere."

A look of trepidation crossed Elsa's face for a minute and her bottom lip stuck out as she thought over what I'd said and weighed her options. She was loyal to that doll no matter how ugly it was. Loyal to a fault. Another one of my traits. But I *still* knew her ass wasn't mine.

"This some evil shit you doin', Legend," Darin told me.

"Man, shut the hell up!" But as I looked at Elsa, I knew he was right.

"Fine, you can keep that creature you holdin' but everything else gotta go. C'mon."

Her face lit up and I couldn't help but be happy that I was able to change her mood.

"You might be alright with this," Darin smiled at me and I cut my eyes in his direction.

"Well, we'll never know because as soon as I find out who her real daddy is, she's going with his ass. I be damned if I send her back to the bitch who named her after Nicki Minaj."

Darin laughed and we all walked out of the house. When we got to the door, Elsa grabbed my hand and I flinched before snatching it away.

"I'm sorry. It's a habit," I told her when I saw tears come to her eyes. "I'm not used to a Princess wanting to hold my hand because I used to be an ogre."

"Still are," Darin added.

"Nigga, getcho ass in the car and go home to your girl," I said as I closed and locked the door behind us. "And don't go blabbing to her ass about this shit. I need to tell Neesy about this on my own."

Darin laughed as he walked over and jumped in his whip.

"Mum's the word, L."

"'Bullet up ya ass' gone be the word if you keep calling me 'L,'" I shot back as I walked to the car with Elsa.

I glanced at her and felt a stirring in my chest that I'd never felt before. Here I was, a nigga who had never even babysat a jit before, and now I had one looking back at me as if I was supposed to know all the answers.

What the fuck was I gonna do?

Chapter Fifteen

MALIAH

"What the hell is her ass doing?" I whispered to myself as I crept down the hall.

It was damn near three o'clock in the morning and the only reason I was even awake was because the twins were doing somersaults in my stomach and trying their hardest to kick my ass.

Murk got in late from whatever business he had to handle, so I decided to sleep in the guestroom down the hall in order not to wake him. But the twins were determined not to let me sleep. I don't know what it was that I ate that had them so mad at me, but I swore to God if he would let me know, I would never touch it again.

In the middle of my prayers to God for release from my place of misery, I heard my mama fumbling around in her room and I knew she wasn't up to any good. She swore up and down that she wasn't making nightly visits to give some man the booty, but I had my suspicions. Fortunately for me, I was alert and ready to see exactly what she was up to.

When I got to the end of the hall, I peeked out and saw her walking to the door with her purse on her shoulder, wearing a long black coat. Yes, it was a little breezy outside but it has never, ever in my life been cold enough to walk around in Miami wearing a full-body, long ass trench coat. Her ass looked like she was getting ready to meet up with Keanu Reeves in the Matrix. Who did she think she was fooling?

Opening my mouth, I was going to bust her right then but I thought twice. Maybe it was the fact that the twins weren't giving me peace that made me want to climb to another level of petty. But whatever it was, it helped me make up my mind. I was going to follow her ass. I already knew what she was up to. Now I had to know who she was doing it with.

Fifteen minutes later, I was in my car following her and we were all the way in Coral Springs. I made sure to maintain a safe distance so that she wouldn't know she was being followed and decide to head in a different direction. It didn't matter where she went, there was no way that she could tell me she wasn't going to see a man. Her favorite thing to say to me was that nothing was open after midnight but legs. Well, from the looks of things, she was about to make sure her pair of slender chocolate thighs would be one of them. That is, unless I had anything to do with it.

"AH HA!" I exclaimed when I saw her pull into a motel.

A raggedy ass one at that! Scrutinizing it, I curled up my nose in disgust at the place her boo had her traveling to for their booty call. I had thought that she was messing around with the pastor, but that couldn't be. I knew damn well Pastor Charles wouldn't do her like this.

Any man worth shit wouldn't make a woman drive all the way to the other side of town from where she lived, just to meet at this raggedy ass motel.

I'd done a lot of things in my past, but money made it easy for a bitch to forget a lot of things. And one of the things that I was happy to forget is that I'd ever laid up with some no good nigga in some shit that look like this. The outside paint was peeling off the walls and some fiends who looked like they were Alicia's old friends were walking around outside. Loretta's ass needed to be ashamed of herself. Hell, even at Motel 6, they always keep the damn light on for you! This nasty ass spot she was in only had one working street lamp outside and it was dim as hell. However, it provided just enough light for the crack heads to congregate around and satisfy their habit.

"This some bullshit!" I said as I slid into a parking spot and waited for her to get out and knock on whichever door her man was in, so I could break up whatever they thought was about to happen. Hell naw, there was no way I was going to let my mama lay her ass up on these Hepatitis infected sheets. Especially not just so she could bring the shit back to my house. From the looks of this place, my beds would be covered with bed bugs, creatures still undiscovered, and God knows what else in the matter of hours upon her return.

After what felt like forever, she finally opened the door and got out. Keeping my eyes on her, I did the same, but a little faster. By the time she started walking to the door of her low down and dirty lover, I was right behind her with my cock-blocking skills intact.

The door opened before she was even able to knock and when I saw who it was that walked out, I damn near went into labor.

"PASTOR?!" I yelled, not believing my eyes. Blinking, I waited for the image ahead of me to change. I knew it couldn't be Pastor Charles who I was seeing. How dare he try to creep around with my mama in this nasty shit?

"AHH!" my mama screamed and tried to cover her face as if that was going to do anything. Did she really think I couldn't tell who she was?

"Sis—si—si…Sister Maliah!" Pastor Charles gasped when his eyes fell on me.

His light, buttery face flushed red as he adjusted the robe that he had on, holding it as if it was his prayer robe that he wore right before his Sunday sermons.

"Don't 'Sister Maliah' me now! What your cheap ass doing over here with my mama?!"

"Maliah Michele!" my mama exclaimed in a reprimanding tone.

I held up my hand to stop her. She couldn't say shit to me now. What she needed to do was to get off her high horse because not only was she sneaking out of *my* house to go give up the booty to the pastor, but she also allowed him to drag her to a crack motel to do it!

"Cheap?" Pastor Charles repeated, frowning at me like he didn't know what I was talking about.

"YES, CHEAP! As in 'you ain't worth shit for this!'"

Walking by him, I pushed up into the room and almost fainted from the smell of mildew and the stale smell of sex and body odors.

"What the hell is this?!" I asked when I saw that he'd laid out strawberries and other chocolate-covered goodies on a table near the bed. He even had the audacity to have rose petals on the bed. The bed that was covered with burn marks from cigarettes and whatever else the crack heads and prostitutes who frequented the place had put on it.

"Oh God," I said holding my stomach when I saw movement on the other side of the room. "Oh God, was that a rat?! Oh God, please save me. No, just take me now!"

A metallic taste came into my mouth and my stomach churned. Then one of the twins kicked hard as if he or she was trying to tell me to get my ass up out of the room.

"Mama, how the hell you let his ass bring you here for a booty call? He don't respect you enough to put you up in a five-star hotel?! Shit… two stars would have been better than this shit!" I fumed, shouting so loud that Pastor Charles went to close the door. "Hell naw! You ain't about to close me up in here! We need the air…Oh God, I need the air. I'mma puke! Oh, Go—"

My stomach lurched and I had to cover my mouth to stop from throwing up.

"Maliah! You need to go home and stay out my business! Why did you follow me here? I'm grown!" Loretta said with her hands on her hips as if she scared me.

"Yes, you real grown and doing some nasty ass grown shit!" I countered, still rubbing my belly as a sharp pain went through it. I gritted my teeth through it until the pain subsided. "This shit so disgusting I'm having contractions. God help me, please!"

As if summoned, Pastor Charles walked forward with his hand out, ready to lay hands on my belly, and started praying.

"Dear God—"

"Don't you pray for me, satan!" I yelled as I batted his hand away. "I don't need you to go to God for me for shit!"

"MALIAH, stop cursing in front of the pastor!" my mama had the audacity to say as she held her hand to her chest in shock. "I didn't raise you that way!"

"Well, who did?!" I shot back. "And who raised you to be okay with rubbing your ass up and down these cum-stained sheets?! And he *ain't* no pastor! He's a pimp and done brought you into the whorehouse!"

"My word!" Pastor Charles gasped.

"Your word ain't shit, Charles!" I yelled as I doubled over in pain once again. "You is *nasty*…you is nasty and everybody should know it! Bringing my mama here to lay where the crack heads lay! Oh Jesus, give me the strength to strangle his ass, please!"

My phone rang and I tried to reach down to grab it as Pastor Charles fell into prayer while my mama continued to reprimand me for my bad language. I couldn't get over this shit. How in the hell did he convince the most judgmental mama in the world to go for this? Love was a hell of a drug. If I didn't learn that with my relationship with Danny, I was damn sure learning it now.

"Murk," I breathed heavily into the phone, still feeling nauseated. I had to get the hell out of that motel. If I didn't, I wasn't going to make it.

"Li, where da fuck you at?! I heard you creeping out the bed and shit but I ain't know you was leaving the house! Don't make me swerve up on you again, nigga! Tell me where da fuck you at and who you with!"

"Oh God..." I said as I tried to breathe, unable to answer him as I attempted to swallow down the bile that rose up at the back of my throat.

"WHAT DA FUCK YOU DOIN' THAT GOT YOU OUT OF BREATH AND SHIT?!" he yelled, sounding like he was moving around the house. "While you praying to God, you better ask Him to get to your ass before I do!"

I heard the sound of a gun cocking through the phone and it brought me back to my senses.

"Murk, I'm not with no other nigga, calm down! I followed Loretta's nasty ass out the house...I had to see who she was meeting with. She giving it up to Pastor Charles in the nastiest motel I ever seen in my life. I need oxygen, bae. It's crack heads over here! She got bats swinging in the room. I swear, even Alicia wouldn't lay up in this shit."

There was silence and then, all of a sudden, laughter filtered in as Murk roared on the other line. Pulling the phone away, I stared at it, trying to figure out what was so damn funny.

"That's what your ass get for being so damn nosey! I told you to stay out of her business!" he yelled and I scowled, gritting my teeth to stop myself from cursing his ass out. I should have hung up right in his face.

"Murk, this shit ain't funny! It's rats in here!"

"Nigga, get your ass back in the car and come home! Let them grown ass people do what the fuck grown people do! It ain't your business what Ma wanna do and who she wanna do it with," Murk countered, still laughing. But I didn't see shit funny.

"Bye, Murk," I said, pressing the red button on the screen. I was done with his ass for life. He was supposed to be on my side but instead, he was having the laugh of the century at my expense.

"Listen, I—the only reason I brought her here is because no one would know us," Pastor Charles tried to explain to me.

"Tell that shit to somebody else," I told him, holding my hand up in his face. "There are a lot of places you could have taken her that wouldn't have her coming back to my house with fleas. There is no excuse for this shit. I've been going to church like I promised God I would every Sunday and giving my lil' coins in the offering, and this the best you can do for my mama?! Then you have the audacity to hide her like she ain't worth shit. Do you even take her on real dates?"

The way they both looked down at their feet told me all I needed to know.

"That's what I thought," I said, giving both of them a look of disgust. "So I'll leave and let y'all do what you wish because my husband asked me to. But he didn't ask me not to be petty, so guess what?"

Turning around, I fluffed the covers and knocked all the rose petals off the bed as my mama gasped from behind me. Then I walked over to the strawberries and chocolate covered fruit, peeled the plastic back and stuffed a handful in my mouth, and I tucked the rest of the tray under my arm.

"Thanks for the treats, Charles. Y'all have a nice night. Loretta, make sure you take a steaming hot bath before you come back, and expect for me to hose you down before you walk in the house," I finished as I walked out and let the door slam behind me.

As soon as I got outside, I spat the strawberries out onto the cracked cement ground. As hungry as I was, I couldn't even stomach it because of how disgusting everything I'd just seen was. I really couldn't believe this shit.

*****

"Mama, we going to see our daddy today?" Shadaej asked me, startling me out of my thoughts.

On the outside, I appeared to be calmly packing lunchboxes for the kids, mainly because I didn't trust Danny to feed them on his own, but in the inside I was seething and my stomach was twisted with worry. The last thing I wanted to do was drop the kids off at Danny's for the weekend, but I had to. Their clothes were packed and I was scheduled to get them all to where he was staying in less than an hour, but I couldn't get my mind to wrap around the idea of letting them go.

"Yes," I replied to Shadaej through my teeth, trying to keep my tears at bay. "Yes, you're going to your daddy for the weekend."

"YAY!" she exclaimed, punching her fist in the air.

LeDejah ran up behind her, obviously after being around the corner ear hustling on our conversation.

"YAY, we're going to see our daddy...we're going to see our daddy!" she sang while jumping up and down next to her older sister.

DeJarion came in not much longer, not fully understanding what was going on, but happy to join in with his sisters as they sang and cheered.

"Go get your shoes on so we can go," I told them with a sigh. Before I could barely finish my sentence, they'd already taken off down the hall to get ready to go.

Leaning over the counter, I ran my hand over my face and sighed once again. Then checked the clock to see how much time we had to drive to Fort Lauderdale. Fifteen minutes.

"What's good, shawty?"

The sound of Murk's voice made my heart jump with excitement, even in the midst of my mental turmoil. Just knowing that he was there did something to me. He always made me feel better…no matter how crazy he was sometimes.

"I'm makin' it. Tryin' anyways," I replied with a weak smile.

Moving forward, he wrapped his arms around me and kissed me on the forehead.

"Don't worry about shit. You know I got you…You're mine, Li. That mean there ain't shit that you gotta worry about. For as long as I'm living, I'll work hard just to see you smile, okay?"

I leaned into him and nodded my head, instantly feeling the honesty in what he said. When you had a strong man leading you, it was easy to trust in his words and know for a fact that his actions measured up to every word he said. With Danny, I always doubted every word that came out his mouth. But Murk was just as real as they came. If he said that I didn't have to worry and everything would be fine, then I knew that's what it was and he would make sure of it.

"Where's Ma?" he said once he'd released me.

Shrugging, I cut my eyes at him and grunted as I zipped up the kids' lunchboxes.

"I have no idea. I guess she's still at the fleabag motel with *her man*," I told him, my voice laced with sarcasm and disdain. "I still can't get over that shit from last night."

Chuckling, Murk leaned on the wall and stared at me, his hazel eyes catching the light in the kitchen and making them glimmer which usually made my knees weak. But after bringing up my mama, I was much too pissed to be aroused. She hadn't showed up, called, or texted me since I caught her with the pastor, and I wasn't the least bit concerned.

"How you gone get mad at a grown woman for doing what grown women do? The pastor's wife is dead, right? Who cares they fuckin'? Hell, pastors need love too."

Murk continued to laugh at his own joke even after I glared at him.

"It's not about the fact that she is sleeping with someone. It's about the fact that my *whole life* she's talked down on me and made me feel like shit about the type of men I've chosen and how they've treated me, and then she goes and dips off with a man who does the same shit!

When I got with you she was all like 'oh, you finally managed to get somebody who cares to treat you right', then I find out that she's doing the same damn thing she used to make me feel guilty about! Talking about how I was just giving my pussy away to any nigga who whispered sweet nothings in my ear...what the hell she think she's doing?!"

I hadn't even realized that I was crying until Murk walked forward and wiped the tears from my eyes. Backing away, he kissed my cheeks and then held my face in his hands.

"You've got to let that shit go, Li. What she was tellin' you was right, even if what she's doing isn't right...but you gotta allow muhfuckas to make their own damn mistakes. She ain't tell you no lie...them niggas before me didn't deserve you. And I should fuck their asses up for treating you like shit back in the day, but I'mma let that shit go on the strength they didn't know who future wife they was fuckin' with."

I laughed when he said that, and Murk reached down and lifted my chin so that I was looking him in his eyes.

"From what you told me, your mama said a lot of fucked up shit to you back in the day, but you ever think it was because she saw you dealing with the same demons that she couldn't get rid of? Parents want the best for their kids. I know I don't want my shorties making the same fucked up decisions I made, na'mean?"

Sniffling, I rubbed my eyes and nodded my head. He was right... as usual, and his ass knew it, judging from the pompous look on his face.

"We ready!" Shadaej yelled out as she ran into the kitchen with her brother and sister trailing behind her, all of them fully dressed and ready to go. The girls even had their little Michael Kors bags that Murk had bought them on their shoulders. My eyes teared up as I looked at them like they were going to be gone forever rather than only a couple days.

"Aye, I got something for y'all," Murk said, reaching into his pocket. He pulled out two cellphones and handed one to each of the girls. Then he pulled out a play phone and handed it to DeJarion, who immediately smiled after frowning, thinking he was left out.

"Y'all remember my number, right?" Both girls nodded their heads. DeJarion mimicked his sisters, his eyes moving back and forth between them and Murk's face.

"Say it for me," he told them and I watched with awe as both of the girls recited his number together.

"If anything happens, I want you to call me. Okay?"

They all nodded their heads. Murk smiled and watched as the girls happily stuffed their phones in their purses and walked away. DeJarion gleefully popped his right in his mouth, instantly covering it with drool.

"Why you didn't make them memorize my number, too?" I asked, punching him lightly in the arm.

Frowning, Murk rubbed the spot I punched and looked at me like I'd spoken in a foreign language.

"Why would I? Any time something happens, you don't do shit but cry, holler and yell for me to fix it!"

"That's the hormones, Murk! You know I don't be crying all the time!" I rolled my eyes and grabbed my purse and the keys. Pushing past him, I nodded to the kids to follow me out the door.

Walking behind me, Murk just had to make sure he got the last word in.

"Hell naw, don't blame yo' craziness on my jits! Yo' ass was puttin' pressure on a nigga before you was pregnant," he joked, making me roll my eyes again.

Waving him off with my hand, I was almost out the door when he grabbed me by the arm and stopped me from leaving.

"You sure you don't want me to come with you?" he asked me and I shook my head quickly.

"No, I can handle this on my own," I told him.

Leaning over, I kissed him lightly on the lips and turned around to leave, hoping like hell he didn't see the doubt in my eyes.

Could I really handle this on my own?

Chapter Sixteen

LEGEND

I was used to people staring at me. The shit happened all the time. But what I wasn't used to was people staring at me because I had a little girl sitting at my side, singing to herself and holding the ugliest damn Barbie doll on the face of the planet.

"Yo, is anybody gonna ask it or do I have to?" Quan said after about three minutes of me sitting down on the bleachers next to him, Dame and Murk.

"I ain't asking shit because I know my damn eyes ain't seeing what the fuck I think they seein,'" Murk said with ease, as he popped some popcorn in his mouth and made an obvious attempt to ignore Elsa who was sitting right next to him humming loudly. She was in her own world. Her hair was still all over her head, but she looked a thousand percent better than she did when I'd first gotten her, now that she was sporting some new shit I'd bought her on the way to the rec center.

"Dame?" Quan pushed, nodding pointedly towards Elsa with his head.

Dame hesitated like he wasn't going to say a thing and then his eyes went down to her. Sighing, he shook his head.

"Hell yeah I'mma ask because I gotta know in case we gotta fix this shit later on. Legend, who baby you kidnapped?"

"I ain't kidnap no shorty. Somebody dropped her ass off at my condo. How the fuck they knew I was there, I don't even know."

"What?" Quan started. He stood up and walked in front of me, pointing his eyes at Elsa. "So she supposed to be yours or something? She looks like you…but who the hell would trust Leith with a child?!"

"The same muhfucka who named her daughter Onika Miraj Dumas," I countered.

"That's fucked up," Murk chimed in. "What you gone do with it?"

"Nigga, you the family man! You tell me what I do with her ass other than throwing her food every now and then? Hell, her ass still in diapers."

"Aw, hell naw!" Quan flung his hands in the air. "Who the fuck supposed to change that stinky shit!"

"It's not a diaper! It's a pulls up!" Elsa yelled angrily all of a sudden. I hadn't even realized she was paying attention to us.

"Nigga, that's a diaper!" Quan argued back at her.

"It's a pulls up for if I have a 'aks cedent', stoopid!" Elsa shot back with her face curled up in a scowl that I knew all too well. It looked like the same one I made damn near on the daily. Silence loomed as we all stared at her.

"Hell to the fuck naw. Legend, you got a jit," Murk said finally.

"I keep tellin' muhfuckas she ain't mine! I don't respect hoes enough to give them my seed. From the way her mama treats her, I know for a fact if we ever fucked around, I shot my shit off on her ass. Fuck I look like bustin' in a bitch who name her kid after a plastic rapper with ass shots? Not Legend," I informed them all, absolutely forgetting that Elsa was sitting right next to me.

Even if she was listening, it was something she needed to hear. If it turned out that she was my daughter, I would want her to know what niggas said about hoes like her mama so she would never turn into one.

"Stop talkin' like that around the shorty, nigga. She might repeat what you sayin'," Dame advised.

"And on top of that, Nicki Minaj is fine as hell. Say something else about my wife-to-be and I won't be able to pardon that shit, ya feel me?" Quan joked. I waved him away and refocused my attention on the game, as they continued to clown about me having Elsa with me.

"For real though, Legend," Murk said finally. "What you gone do with her?"

He asked the question that I'd been asking myself ever since I came to terms with the fact that I was left with her, and couldn't give her right back to the dumb chick who had scratched her damn name off Elsa's birth certificate.

"I'm getting a blood test ASAP. If she's not mine, I'm finding her mama so I can give her to her real daddy," I told him. I glanced at Elsa and saw that she was watching the basketball players on the court with intensity. The ugly doll was lying across her lap with the bald spot on the back of her head pointed upwards. Elsa caught me looking and frowned before placing her finger to her lips and shushing me.

"She's sleeping. We gots to be a-quiet."

"A-quiet?" I quizzed with one eyebrow lifted. She nodded her head factually like she was teaching me something, and then focused back on the game.

"What you gone do about Neesy?" Murk asked, again repeating a question I'd asked myself a few times. "If it were Li, she'd fuck my ass up for bringing a lil' midget home."

"If Elsa is mine, Neesy is going to have to come to terms with it. Hell, her sister did!"

"Neesy is not her sister," Murk chuckled, nudging me in the arm.

"Hell naw, she isn't. Tan's evil. So if she can accept a baby, I know Neesy can," I told him.

Once again, I let my attention fall on Elsa. Omega hit a three-point shot and the crowd roared. Elsa shot her tiny little arms in the air and hooted right with them as if she knew what was going on. I couldn't help but smile at her. She was a cute kid. *Someone else's* cute kid though…because she wasn't mine.

"Ah shit, look who it is," I heard Murk say from beside me. He nudged me again with his elbow and I turned around to see who it was.

"The fuck Martinez doing here?" Quan asked as we all glared at her.

She was dressed down in jeans and a tank top with some heels on. As we all silently watched her strut in our direction, her ebony skin glowing under the fluorescent lights, I knew we were thinking the same thing. Agent Martinez was fine as hell when she took off all that police shit she usually wore. Her hair, that was usually tucked in a bun, was loose and cascading down her shoulders, showing off its length as well highlighting her nicely toned arms. She had hips for days and swung them just right in her painted on jeans that had every nigga for miles focused on everything below the belt.

She had it going on, I had to admit. But I couldn't stand her ass. Once again, she had found her way into my shit.

"She's probably here because she couldn't find me back at the crib since I ain't been there. I'm tired of her ass watchin' me," I spat as my eyes locked with hers. I glared at her but she didn't flinch and didn't look away either. She held my gaze the entire time as she sashayed over in my direction.

"I'mma let you handle this bitch before I find myself locked up for another fuckin' murder," Murk said as he stood up and walked away.

Quan and Dame followed behind him. As Quan walked by, Martinez's eyes left mine for only a second as she glanced at Quan, giving him a sideways look. She knew that Quentin had a twin but I guess it was her first time seeing him.

"Hello, Leith," she greeted me as she sat down beside me.

Cutting my eyes at her, I glared right into her face before turning back to the game. She smirked back at me, seemingly amused by how much I couldn't stand her ass.

I picked up Elsa and placed her in between the both of us. I saw people watching us and the last thing I wanted them to think was that

I was cheating on Shanecia with a fucking federal agent.

Shit, they gone think Elsa is ours, I thought and reached out to grab Elsa and move her. Then I stopped suddenly.

Fuck what they think, I thought to myself. *And if anybody say shit about it, I'll put a hot one in their bitch ass.*

"What's your name, cutie?" Martinez asked, looking down at Elsa.

I scowled at her, wanting to tell her not to talk to my daughter. But then I remembered she wasn't mine and would be gone soon, so I turned my attention back to the game and ignored both of them.

"Princess Elsa," she answered without hesitation.

"Princess Elsa?"

"Yeah, my daddy told me that I could call me that," she explained, pointing her little finger at me.

"The hell I told you about talking to strangers, Elsa?!" I reminded her and she clamped her mouth closed. Her shoulders drooped down and her bottom lip poked out.

"Ah shit, I know your ass ain't 'bout to cry! Fuck!" I cursed, growing even more agitated by the second.

The agitation multiplied by fifty when I heard Martinez chuckling to my side.

"Wow," she said after she was done with the shits and giggles. "Is that how you talk to your daughter?"

"She ain't mine," I gritted through my teeth. "Some bitch dropped her off at my house and left. Why don't you do your fuckin' job and help me find her? Isn't child abandonment a crime?"

"Not when you drop the kid off with her father."

I squeezed my hands into fists to stop myself from grabbing at Martinez's throat. How many fuckin' times did I have to tell people that Elsa wasn't my kid before they would believe me?

"I gotsta go pee!" Elsa whined all of a sudden. I peered over at her and saw that she was twisting around on the seat with her face balled up as if she was in pain.

"The bathroom is back there to the right," I told her, pointing back towards the entrance of the rec center.

"You can't let her go there by herself!" Martinez shot out with an incredulous look on her face as she frowned at me. I shrugged and turned back towards the game. Omega was doing his thing on the court. Whatever part of hell Alpha's backstabbing ass was in, I'm sure he was proud.

"Ugh!" Martinez grumbled with annoyance before snatching Elsa up from the seat. "I'll take her to the bathroom!"

"Yeah and after that, take her to her real daddy too!"

She sucked her teeth and then stormed away, but not before rolling her eyes at me and giving me a 'you ain't shit' look that made me laugh. One thing was for sure: you could be the Feds or you could be a project bitch, it didn't matter; when Black women got an attitude, they all did the same damn thing.

As if on cue, my own Black woman with an attitude texted me at the very moment that I'd began to think about her.

I miss you. You left too soon.

I hit her right back. *I'll be back soon. Don't worry. Miss u 2.*

Martinez and Elsa came back right as I pushed the phone in my pocket. I looked up right into Elsa's bright face. She was grinning at me, as she walked back holding Martinez's hand.

"I go pee all by myself!" she chimed happily as soon as she sat down beside me.

"Good, because I ain't changing no diapers," I reminded her.

"They *not* diapers!"

"Whatever."

The fourth quarter began and we all sat in silence watching the game. Every time anyone made a basket, Elsa roared along with the crowd. It didn't matter which team it was, she got excited. I tried to tell her that she had to pick a team and stick to it, but she didn't hear a word I was saying.

"Stop that shit," I told her again. "If you rooting for every damn nigga on the team, that makes you a THOT. You gotta pick a team and stick with that *one* team. Get it?"

She screwed her face up at me and the turned back to the game as if I hadn't said a word.

"A THOT?" Martinez repeated, looking at me like she was amused.

I glanced at her. I knew that look. As much as she tried to be Agent Hardass, it was falling through. She'd made the mistake of taking off her uniform and some of her professionalism had went away with it. It was easy to act like a cop when you looked like one because people treated you like one to the point that you could never forget. But she was in plain clothes and was a bit relaxed. Too relaxed.

"Yes…THOT. You never heard of one?" I asked before explaining further. "THOT. 'That hoe over there'…?"

"I know what THOT means. I was just wondering why you would tell a child something like that." She laughed, showing off her perfectly white teeth. "Like, who *does* that?!"

"You won't find many niggas who operate how I do. I'm a Legend. Which reminds me…stop with that Mr. Dumas and that Leith shit, okay?"

"You have a problem with me calling you by your name? I didn't think that was something people got offended by," she joked with sarcasm. She placed her hand under her chin to hold her face as she stared at me.

"That's *not* my name," I corrected her. "And I keep tellin' you I'm not like any other nigga. Stop trying to figure me out because you won't. They call me Legend and I didn't give myself that name, the streets did because of how I move."

"Oh," she replied pensively. "You always this cocky and full of shit?"

She smirked and I cut my eyes at her, slightly amused at the way that she spoke to me without fear. She said things that would normally get the shit knocked out of her had she just been any other broad in the streets.

"Hell yeah," I replied with a tacit nod.

"I can dig it," she replied back to me and I glanced back at her once more. She turned to the game as I scrutinized her but I could tell by looking at her that she wasn't paying attention to shit. She knew that I was studying her and I could tell by the way that her breath slowed down, to almost the point that her breathing was unnoticeable. Her lips parted slightly and her eyelids seemed to be drunk as they opened and closed more slowly.

I knew it, I thought with a smirk on my face. *I could fuck her ass and all this shit would go away. All she needs is some dick to set her stuck up ass right.*

Testing her, I leaned in close, pushing my lips close to her neck. She sucked in a subtle breath, impossible to notice to the untrained eye, but kept her eyes on the game as I continued to get closer. My lips grazed her neck and she suddenly gasped before exhaling slowly. But she didn't pull away.

But I did.

My message to her had been delivered and now I was done. I knew that I could fuck her if I wanted to and now she knew the same. It was time to go.

"I'll holla. C'mon, Elsa," I told her as I snatched her ass up from the bench.

"But Daddy, it's not over!" she cried but I ignored her.

Smiling, I chucked Martinez the deuces and walked away, leaving her still sitting there clenching her knees together and trying to ignore her wet panties.

Chapter Seventeen

SHANECIA

"Negative," I said as I looked at the third pregnancy test that I'd taken since I'd gotten up.

I didn't want to say anything to Legend, but I was feeling strange and I had been for a while. Not only was I nauseated more often than not, but I had a blaring headache that wouldn't go away. At first, I thought it might have been those pills I was taking for anxiety, so I tossed those and waited for the symptoms to go away, but they didn't.

My nipples felt hard and hurt to the point that my breasts were red in color. From all these symptoms, I just knew that I had to be pregnant, but every test that I took said the same thing. Negative.

"So are you pregnant?!" Cush asked, barging into my room.

When Legend left, she and Alani came over to keep me company. It didn't take Cush's nosey ass long to find me puking my entire heart out into the toilet and ask whether or not I was pregnant. From there, I confided in her about everything that I'd been feeling and she went with me to buy the tests.

"No," I told her with a shrug. "I don't get it. Every test says negative but I know something isn't right."

The disappointment was obvious on Cush's face. She wanted me to be pregnant along with everyone else I knew. Maliah was always trying to convince me that it would be the greatest thing on Earth if I got pregnant while she was so that our kids could grow up together. I entertained the idea every now and then, but they were trying to convince the wrong person. Legend was the one who didn't want to hear shit about kids.

"I think I need to go to the doctor. I may be coming down with something," I said, sighing as I tossed the tests in the trash and walked out of the bathroom.

"You want me to go with you? I don't have anything to do until Alani gets back from her chapter meeting with her sorors later on."

Pursing my lips, I looked at her not wanting to readily admit that I was afraid and did want someone to go with me. I was so used to always giving myself to others who needed me that I wasn't quite sure how to react when I was on the receiving end of need.

Cush picked up on my struggle instantly.

"Let me put on my clothes now," she said as she turned to walk away. "Neesy, there is nothing wrong with asking for help sometimes. Damn...I am going to be your sister soon!"

I let out a nervous chuckle as she walked into the guestroom to get dressed and I started to do the same. Part of me wanted to call Legend to tell him how I was feeling, but he had enough going on and I didn't want to bother him.

"You ready?" Cush asked me about 10 minutes later.

I was fully dressed and staring at myself in the mirror, trying to ignore the looming feeling that something wasn't right. Call it a woman's intuition or clairvoyance…I just knew bad news was coming.

"I'm ready," I told her, taking a quick glance at how flawless she was able to make herself look in less than 15 minutes.

"You wanna call Legend?" she asked me and I shook my head 'no'.

"I don't want to worry him with this and find out nothing is wrong," I said, which was more of a hope than anything else. I didn't feel that it was, but I still hoped that everything was fine anyways.

*****

The moment the doctor walked inside of the room, I knew something was up. Cush had managed to convince me for the most part that I had nothing to worry about, but from the grim expression on Dr. Mitchell's face, I knew that things were just as bad as I'd thought they were.

Initially, I'd tried to make an appointment with my normal physician but she was on vacation, so I had to go to urgent care. Then urgent care referred me to Grady, saying that they didn't have the equipment for some of the tests they needed to run. So here I was… waiting on the news. And from the way that Dr. Mitchell walked in the room looking like someone had died, I was already positive it wouldn't be good.

"Okay, Ms. J—"

"You can just call me Neesy," I interrupted him, blurting out a response birthed from sheer anxiety. I was nervous as hell and fidgeting with my own fingers, as I sat waiting for him to tell me what was wrong. My face had a sheen of sweat over it although it was pretty cool in the room. Cush was at my side and although she was trying to keep it cool, I could pick up on her vibes and I knew she was low-key tripping about how Dr. Mitchell was acting as well.

"Neesy...according to the MRI and imaging tests that we conducted, you have a rather large mass in your breasts. I will have to do a biopsy to know for sure but—"

"Oh God," I said quietly, expelling a rush of air from my lungs. Leaning over, I held onto the edge of the examination table I was seated on as I tried to steady myself.

"Oh God, I have cancer." Tears came to my eyes.

"I can't say it's cancer for sure...no one can say that until we conduct another test, so I need you to stay positive," Dr. Mitchell continued. "We can schedule a biopsy for as soon as you wish. All we have to do is—"

As he continued to speak, my mind traveled to a distant place where everything that was happening was a dream. It was a place where I'd taken a pregnancy test and found out that I was actually pregnant. I told Legend, my only worry being that he would be upset. Then after he convinced me that he wasn't angry and had been lying the whole time and really wanted a baby, my next worry would only be that I didn't want to have a baby out of wedlock so I would force him to marry me before the baby was born so we could do things the right way.

Why couldn't these be my real worries? After all that I've been through, why did I now have to worry about cancer?

"Neesy?" I heard Cush call me, her voice elevated like she'd been saying my name for a while. "Neesy...can you hear me?"

When I finally pulled myself out of the reality that I wished for and returned to the reality that was, I realized that my face was covered with tears. I'd been crying and didn't even know it. Dr. Mitchell had his hand on my knee, patting it while assuring me with his mouth that everything was alright.

"You have to remain positive," he told me. "I've seen this happen plenty of times and it was nothing."

Turning to Cush he said, "Take care of her."

"I will," she said as she reached out and pulled me up under her arm into a genuinely caring embrace. "You're going to be okay."

With tears running down my cheeks, I nodded my head and hugged her back. But, deep down, I didn't think it was. This seemed like it was the beginning of something bad, instead of the ending. The mass added to the way I'd been feeling the past few days, and the throwing up told me that I needed to prepare myself because things were definitely not going to be okay.

But how in the world was I going to tell Legend?

LEGEND

"I don't want to eat that!" Elsa shouted as I stared at her.

In two seconds, I was about to plop her little ass right outside of my neighbor's spot with a letter that she was his kid so he could deal with her ass.

"What the hell you wanna eat then?"

"Beanie weenies!" she told me, crossing her arms in front of her chest and kicking her hip out to the side as if she was the one calling the shots.

"No restaurant 'round here serve that shit! And I don't want you puttin' anything called 'weenies' in your mouth ever! You got that?!"

Scrunching up her face, she gave me a look like I'd lost my mind but I didn't care. Leave it to her hoe ass mama to be serving her daughter 'weenies' all the damn time. I couldn't wait until I found out who she was.

"What's your mama's name?" I quizzed, looking at her sideways. She pulled her lips into a tight line as if someone had already warned her not to tell anyone.

"You tell me what her name is and I'll get you some beanie...hot dogs," I said slowly, abruptly stopping myself from saying 'weenies'. "I'll get you some pork 'n beans...that's what they are called."

"Food first!" she demanded with her chin jutted out at me.

"Hell naw, you can't hustle a hustler, lil' girl!" I told her, squaring my stance as I glared down at her.

I was fully aware that I probably looked crazy as hell, standing in the dining area of my condo in a full stand-off with a four-year-old, but I didn't care. She wasn't about to run shit. That was my damn job.

"Food first!" she repeated even louder.

Bending down, I got to her level so I was looking at her straight in her eyes.

"Listen," I began as I pointed my finger at her chest. "You don't run shit, I run shit!"

"No, *I* run shit!"

"Watch yo' damn mouth!"

"No, you watch yo' damn mouth!"

My face fell as I looked at the tight expression on hers. Her ass wasn't budging a bit and she wasn't scared at all. I'd finally met my match and Princess Elsa was it.

The doorbell rang and I stood up, still focusing on her as she stood before me with her hands on her hips, looking like somebody's mama. Apparently, she thought she was mine.

"You lucky that doorbell rang! It saved your ass," I told her.

"No, it saved *your* ass," she replied back.

"You right," I admitted as I walked to answer the door. "But we gone talk about your nasty ass mouth when I get back."

I looked out through the peephole and wasn't even surprised at who it was that I saw. Sighing, I opened the door.

"If you don't want her to have a nasty mouth, you should stop cursing in front of her," Agent Martinez told me as she walked inside without bothering to wait for me to invite her in.

"Your ass better not be here on business, bustin' up in my shit without a fuckin' warrant," I said as I backed out of the way and fully let her in.

I wasn't the least bit worried even if she was snooping. I wasn't stupid enough to keep any kind of incriminating evidence at any spot where I laid my head. The only thing she would find if she searched my spot was money. But every damn body knew Legend was hood rich. Finding money didn't prove shit.

"I'm not here on official business," Martinez admitted once we arrived in the living room, which was right across from the kitchen where Elsa was.

I glanced inside and saw that she had sat down and was pushing around the steak and potatoes I'd bought for her with her fork. Chuckling, I shook my head. She would rather be defeated than to snitch on her mama. As I watched her, she turned and cut her eyes at me, chomping on the potatoes with her head held high. She gave me a look that told me that I'd really lost the battle, I just didn't know it yet. She was a trip for real.

"Look…Sarafin, the agent who was killed, she was my friend. She was my *best* friend," Martinez started, pulling my focus from Elsa. "I'm adopted. My parents were murdered and my father, a Cuban federal agent who was investigating their murder, he took me in and raised me as his. I wasn't accepted into the Cuban community because I'm Black.

But Sarafin accepted me from the beginning. She taught me Spanish… she was my friend. She was murdered and I just have to know what happened. I need to be able to make sure she didn't die for nothing."

Martinez had started crying while she was talking, and I couldn't help but feel bad for her. Not because of the stupid ass crying she was doing. Any chick could make herself cry so that shit didn't move me. But I did feel for her when it came to her friend.

To not be accepted and have that one person who looks out for you and demands everyone gives you the respect that you deserve… that was what Murk did for me when we were younger. It was what all of my brothers did, but Murk went above and beyond. He always had my back in a way that was uncanny to anyone who didn't have someone like him in their corner. He didn't give a shit what you thought about him but he wouldn't stand by and let anybody disrespect me. I was his little brother but it was beyond that. In the ghetto, me and my brothers were all we had.

"Listen, I'm sorry for the shit that happened to your friend," I started as I looked at Martinez. "It's fucked up…but, I swear, me, Dame and Murk ain't have shit to do with that. Your friend was fuckin' with Mello…she was in some shit that she shouldn't have been in and a lot comes with that life. But if you're looking for her killer, it ain't me. I don't fuck with the Feds. Period."

Wiping away a tear from her face, Martinez looked up with a soft expression on her face as she nodded her head.

"Okay," she said with a sigh.

"Does this mean you'll stop fuckin' around with me?" I asked her, shooting her a sly grin that I used to give women back in the day. "You fine and all, but I'd be lying if I said you wasn't bad for business."

I licked my lips as I allowed my eyes to fall over her curves. She was fine as fuck, but Shanecia had my heart so no matter how curious I was, I would never go there with Martinez. But I knew the easiest way to sway her would be a little flattery so I went with it. Truth was, she didn't have shit on me and wouldn't find any either. There was a lot of careless muthafuckas she could be locking up if she would stop fucking with me. She needed to focus on them.

Laughing, she nodded her head. "I'll leave you alone...to do whatever it is you do."

Her eyes lingered on me a little longer than she probably wanted them to, because the next thing I heard was a nervous chuckle as she shrugged before clearing her throat.

"What are you going to do about Princess Elsa?" she asked, turning her attention to the dining room table.

"I need a DNA test. I also need to find out who her mother is. Can you help with that?" I inquired, playing with her by making her feel uneasy from the way I was watching her.

"Uh...yeah, I know someone at the hospital who can help with that. I'll set it up and send you the information for when you can come down for the test. I'll take care of it."

"And what about you?"

"Me?" she asked.

"Yeah," I licked my lips and watched as her eyes lowered to take them in. "Who's gonna take care of you?"

Time to seal the deal.

Reaching out, I pulled her in close to me and wrapped my hands around her tiny waist. She didn't fight me for a second. She simply fell into place.

As much as I wanted to say that it was hard to kiss her, it wasn't. I knew I was dead wrong, but I reasoned in my mind that it was what I needed to do in order to get Martinez off my case. I needed to get her wrapped up just enough for her to think that she had a chance, so she could leave me the fuck alone and I could do what I needed to do and go on and live my life with Shanecia.

That wasn't a bad thing, right?

Just as my lips were about to touch hers, my phone rang. It was almost like God was intervening and keeping me from doing some dumb shit. When I saw who it was calling, I knew I was right.

"Neesy?" I asked, answering the call and pulling away from Martinez. She stepped away and tried to get herself together, but I could tell she was slightly disappointed.

"Legend, it's me."

"Cush...what's going on? Where is Neesy...why are you callin' me from her phone?" I inquired in a rushed tone, feeling my heart rate begin to speed up.

I could tell from the sound of Cush's voice that something was wrong, and if something happened to Shanecia while I was over here doing some fucked up shit with Martinez, I would never forgive myself.

"My phone died. Listen! I have something to tell you…it's about Neesy. She doesn't want me to tell you but I don't think it's right that I keep something like this from you."

"Hold on," I interrupted Cush, feeling my heart tightening in my chest. I needed to gauge the seriousness of the situation. "Is this something that's gone make me hop in the whip?"

Cush hesitated for a second and my heart felt like it had been stabbed a million times just that quickly.

"Yes…Yes, I think so," she admitted, sadly.

Turning, I looked at Agent Martinez, wondering if she was gonna be a problem if I tried to leave the city again. One quick look told me that I wouldn't have to worry about her standing in the way ever again. She could barely look me in the eyes. I hadn't even needed to kiss her to seal the deal. And it was a good thing because if something had happened to Shanecia while I was over here doing some shit that would crush her, I wouldn't be able to take the guilt that came with that.

"Explain this shit to me quick, Cush. I'm already on my way."

Chapter Eighteen

TANECIA

"Let me see the baby," my mama asked, holding her hands out to hold Jen.

Smiling, I walked over to her and plopped Jen's fat self right in her hands. She looked right up into my mama's face and a wide grin spread across her face, showing off her cute little dimples. She truly was the prettiest little girl I'd ever seen.

It was Saturday, and we were all hanging out at the house getting ready to eat whatever it was that was smelling good as hell that Darin was cooking on the grill. My mama had finally been approved to leave the rehabilitation facility for a few hours at a time, so we decided it was a good time to invite her, Carol, who was Jenta's mother, and Diane, who was Darin's mother, all over for a cookout to hang out with us and Jen.

Everyone there was trying to make the most of an awkward situation. It was obvious to everyone that Darin and I were having problems doing the blended family thing, but no one wanted to say a thing about it. On top of that, I could tell that Diane really wanted to ask my mama where she fit in the whole equation but hadn't gotten the nerve to do so. However, her stank ass attitude and the way she kept curling up her lips at my mama was getting on my damn nerves. She always thought she was too good for everybody, but I was ready to remind her ass that she came from the heart of the ghetto, too.

"So, Alicia…what have you been up to lately? Haven't seen you since I left the old neighborhood," Diane said, her condescending tone making my toes curl.

Turning my attention to my mama, I knew it was gone be some shit when I saw her straighten her back and mimic Diane's prim and proper posture.

"Oh, Diane," using her best 'proper and upper-class' voice. "I've been just traveling here and there. Used to frequent the crack houses but I've since then gotten my shit together so now I can be bougie like you."

Spewing sweet tea all over the outside deck, Carol immediately started choking and grabbing at her throat, as Diane and I both gasped at my mama's words.

"Mama!" I widened my eyes when she looked in my direction, attempting to silently urge her to behave. But instead, she widened her eyes right back at me, giving me a vicious bug-eye as she shrugged and lifted her hands up as if to say 'What?!'.

"Can you behave, please?!" I asked her through my teeth as she juggled Jen on her lap.

"I was behaving until Diane started acting like she wasn't standing in the same W.I.C. line I was in back in the day. Damn, Diane, I know you heard about where I been! It sure wasn't the Four Seasons! Bougie ass bi—"

"MAMA!"

"Girl, fuck her," my mama scoffed as she rolled her eyes and waved me off with one hand before returning her attention back to Jen.

Absolutely mortified, I stared as she began cooing and goo-gooing in Jen's face, as if Diane wasn't shooting bullets at her from her eyes. I glanced over to where Darin was, silently grilling the meat as if he didn't hear a thing that was going down.

"Honestly, I don't understand why she's here," Diane muttered finally, just as I had begun to pray that we wouldn't have any more issues out of her and my mama.

"I thought this was a cookout for the *grandmothers* to spend time with *our* granddaughter." Diane spat each word out of her mouth with so much venom it was a wonder they didn't scorch her lips coming out.

"I'm here because *my* daughter has been the one helping to take care of *your* grandchild, heffa!" my mama said matter-of-factly, as she held Jen with one hand and pointed her forefinger at Diane with the other.

"You know…the same way that prostitute on the corner used to do for you back in the day when your mammy was getting hit from the back by that old, peg-leg nigga you think might by your daddy!"

Mama jumped up and Carol started choking again, this time on her own spit as she held her hands up to try to keep mama from reaching over to snatch Diane right out of her chair.

"Give me the baby!" I said as I snatched Jen from her arms. "And Mama, sit down! Please, we didn't have y'all come out here for all this!"

"Well, somebody tell Mrs. Ghetto Queen that!" Mama said to me as she sucked her teeth and sat back down in her seat. "Bitch 'bout to run me back to the damn pipe. She get on my damn nerves!"

"How about we talk about something else?" Carol offered as soon as she was able to collect herself. I smiled at her, grateful that she was trying to be the peacemaker, although the other two were acting up.

"So, Jen will be celebrating her birthday in some months…it may be a little early to be talking about it, but do you all have anything planned?" she asked with a smile on her face as she looked back and forth between me and Darin.

A wide grin crossed my face as I handed Jen a toy that she plopped right into her mouth. I had an answer right at the tip of my tongue because I'd been already thinking on her first birthday, even though it was months away.

"Yes, I was planning a few things," I started, feeling my face light up as I pictured the images in my mind. "I was thinking a party here at the house…we could invite everyone who has children in the neighborhood. I checked some prices on bounce houses and found this company that offers them along with a clown and pony rides and—"

"Ho—ho—hold on, Tan," Darin started, finally decided to butt into the conversation. "Pony rides and bounce houses for a child who is turning one?" he asked with one eyebrow raised as he poked at the grill. "You don't think that's a little much? I think we should have something like what we have going on here…of course invite the grandfathers.

Good food and music…cake and ice cream…that's all she needs."

"That's all she needs?" I asked with a frown as I looked at him. He shrugged as an answer to my question.

Chuckling, I rolled my eyes and looked back at Carol, Diane and Mama to continue talking.

"Well, I think for her *first* birthday, she deserves more than a little cake and ice cream. After all, this is a birthday for her and not us. She needs to enjoy it as much as possible!" I reasoned.

Diane glared at me, huffed and rolled her eyes before turning away. Mama nodded in agreement and Carol nervously looked back and forth between me and Darin. I knew that I was crossing the line a little by not backing down and letting it go, but I was tired of always letting things go when it came to Jen.

Darin expected me to never have any input but to also help him raise his daughter. Besides that, he'd told me that he wasn't interested in planning her first birthday and would let me have that. But now he was pulling back on that promise. I couldn't help it. I was furious!

"She will enjoy it!" Darin battled. "What else can a one-year-old want other than cake and ice cream? It's not like she can ride the pony or jump in the bounce house! That shit ain't for her."

"I agree with him," Diane chimed in. "I bought all these gifts for Darin's first birthday and all he wanted to do was play with the boxes."

"Diane, don't lie," Mama said. "I was there, remember? He was playin' with boxes because that's all you gave him. My husband and I bought Darin's only gift because you ain't buy shit! Wasn't no gifts, bitch!"

Ignoring the two of them, I jumped up and turned my full attention on him as I held Jen in my hands.

"Darin, you told me that I could plan Jen's first birthday and that's what I did. Now you want to switch it up on me out of nowhere?" I asked with my eyes narrowed.

"I'm not switching it up on you! You can still plan her birthday all you want. All I'm saying is for *my* daughter, all that shit is too much. You need to scale it back a little," he counted as he dropped his grilling fork and walked around the grill to square up with me. His eyes were flaming with anger and I'm sure mine matched his glare, as he walked towards me with his chin in the air.

"*Your* daughter?" I asked, laughing as I said it. But it was an evil coarse laugh. The kind of laugh that happens when someone has just tried the shit out of you and you was getting ready to either throw hands or read their ass to filth. I didn't know which one I was about to do to Darin, but I was ready for it.

Handing Jen off to Carol as she watched nervously, her eyes panning back and forth between us with her mouth moving as if she were trying to find something to say, I walked forward and bumped my forefinger into Darin's chest as I continued.

"*Your* daughter, huh?" I began. "You mean the same daughter that I take care of? The one whose diapers *I* change? The one who *I* wake up in the middle of the night to feed? You mean the one who *I* dress and take to daycare? The same daycare that *I* was up all night researching to make sure they were certified and wasn't in the papers for killing kids or leaving them in the crib all day?!"

As I continued my voice got louder and louder and I got angrier and angrier. He had pissed me off to the muthafuckin' max.

"Oh, you mean the daughter who *I* schedule doctor's appointments for and make sure that she goes to? The daughter that *I*—"

"We get it, we get it," Diane scoffed from behind me. "You help Darin watch Jen, we hear you. But, in my opinion, that's what you should be doing being that you living here for free. Ain't worked a day in your life since I've known you. Only thing you do is live off men and my son is only your next victim."

"Bitch, don't make me choke you so hard that bird's nest you call a wig flies off your fuckin' head!" Mama shouted, jumping back up and leaning over to grab at Diane. "Ain't the pot callin' the muthafuckin' kettle black?! At least my daughter was giving it up to men who had her driving in Hummers and Range Rovers! You was giving it up back in the day to anyone who wanted it, and all you had was that broke down Ford Pinto that couldn't get you from here to the Aventura Mall!"

"I can't take this shit no more," Carol grumbled from under her breath. "Everybody, CALM DOWN!"

Amazed at the sudden change in her demeanor, all of us turned and focused in on Carol who had placed Jen on the blanket laid out on the floor of the deck, and was standing with her hands on her hips.

"This can't happen like this!" she continued. "Darin, Jenta is gone. And as much as it hurts me that I lost my daughter, I will not have you pushing away the one woman who has stood in her place and proven to be just as good a mother to Jen as Jenta could have been to her own child! From day one, Tanecia has been there and she's done a damn good job. How dare you treat her like she's only a nanny or someone who doesn't care about your child?"

Carol stopped speaking and simply frowned at Darin as if she were waiting for him to respond. Instead of replying, he pushed his hands in his pockets and dropped his head, sheepishly looking at his feet. His ass knew he was wrong for how he treated me.

"What she said!" Mama piped up, needing to put her two cents in.

Then she turned her attention back to Diane who was still sitting with a stank ass look on her face. I was getting tired of her ass my damn self but I wasn't prepared at all for what my mama was about to say.

"And as for *you,* just 'cause your son moved your ass out the ghetto don't mean shit! You need to remember where you came from because you ain't working either. At least my daughter is getting taken care of by *her man!* Here you are leeching off your damn son and wanna talk shit. Go fix that backwards ass wig! You remember I used to be in the church, right? Well, here is a scripture for your ass: 'Ye of no hair are not to disrespect us of good hair'. That mean keep yo' no edges ass mouth closed! Always trying to talk about what you got! Don't act like I don't know what you *ain't* got…and that's edges!"

"My Lord!" Carol exclaimed with her hand to her chest.

"Edges…on your head!" Mama further clarified as if we didn't know what she had been referring to. "You ain't got none, ain't never gone have none."

"You know what? Everybody just go!" Darin said finally. "Just leave! This shit was bogus. Should've known we couldn't invite everyone over here and have a good time. Just go! I'm sorry, Mrs. Washington," he said to Carol in an apologetic tone.

"It's okay, son. One day we'll be able to get together and it'll be fine," she said with her lips pursed, her face displaying the doubt that she held concerning her words.

Leaving them, I walked over to my mama and hugged her tightly.

"I'm sorry, Mama," I told her as I began to walk with her back inside the house. "Let me get my purse and I'll take you back."

"There is nothing for you to apologize for. This was bound to happen." She cut her eyes at Diane who walked by her with her nose high in the air. "You talked to Neesy today?"

Grabbing my purse, I shook my head. "Not today but I did yesterday. She's been pretty distant lately but I don't know why. Legend is up there with her so I know she's fine though. It must just be school getting to her."

Pushing her lips together into a straight line, Mama nodded her head.

"Yeah, she seemed strange with me, too. I hope school is what it is."

Watching her facial expression change, I could tell something was wrong but I waited until we were outside of the house to ask.

"Something happen between you and Neesy?" I inquired once we were in the car.

Looking up, I saw Darin peek out the blinds just as I was backing out of the yard, and I resisted the urge to give him the middle finger. I couldn't wait to get back home so I could ignore his ass. Petty, I know. But I didn't care.

"A lot has happened," she admitted in a sad tone. "Last time I saw my baby before going to rehab, I whipped her with a belt. Since then, she's called me and visited me a few times, but things have changed. Her and I used to be so close and it was me and you that didn't get along. I'm glad I'm close to you now, but I don't know what to do about Neesy. I don't know if she'll ever forgive me…"

Her voice trailed off and I glanced over, catching her wiping a tear from her eye. Reaching out, I patted her knee, hoping that it would give her some sense of comfort.

"Neesy is a forgiving person, Mama. But you know she needs time. It was a shock to her to come home and see you the way you were, so she's just trying to get her mind together. She'll come around, I promise. Just keep getting better."

With a weak smile, Mama nodded her head and wiped at her face again.

"I hope you're right," she said.

"I know I am."

What I'd said about Shanecia was right and Mama knew it. She was always the forgiving one who could never hold a grudge, even if she tried to. I was the one who allowed my emotions and anger to take over.

All I could do was pray that I could keep them at bay long enough to deal with this issue I had with Darin. But truth was, after how he'd acted at the cookout, I wasn't positive that what was happening with us could be fixed.

Chapter Nineteen

SHANECIA

"Neesy, you have to eat," Cush said as she watched me push around the food on my plate. "I didn't cook for you to just babysit it on your plate. Plus, you need your strength because..."

"Because of the cancer?" I finished for her, dropping my fork down on the table. "I need my energy and strength in order to fight the cancer, right?"

Cush shook her head but she wasn't able to hide the look on her face. The look of pity and fear. It told me everything I needed to know about her thoughts, regardless to what her mouth said.

"That's not what I was going to say," Cush replied with an uneasy look still showing through her eyes. "You'll need your strength for whatever comes next. And you'll also need your love ones around you to help you deal with this. Take it from me...it's no fun dealing with major shit all on your own."

Biting my lip, I looked away and thought on what she said for a few seconds. As much as I wanted Legend by my side, I couldn't bring myself to make him feel like I did at that moment. I was caught between knowing and not knowing.

My entire future was uncertain at the moment and all I could do was wait, hope and pray. I couldn't put the burden of worry on him. It would be selfish of me to do that to him because the only one who would feel comfort from him knowing would be me. I would feel at peace in his arms and he would feel like he had when Mello had taken me: helpless to save the woman he loved.

"I don't want to do that to him," I told Cush, wiping away a lone tear that had traveled down my cheeks. "I want Legend to be here, but I love him too much to burden him with this. He's been through enough."

"And so have you! Don't you know my brother at all?! If you did, you would know that he'd fuck us all up if he knew we held this shit from him!" Cush shot back with a frown on her face. Then she sat all the way back in her chair and the frown was placed by a bold look of defiance and stubbornness. It mirrored the many expressions Legend made.

"And that's why I told him everything," she said as if it was nothing. "He'll be here in a few minutes. He texted me about five minutes ago and said his plane had landed and he was on his way."

"CUSH! Why would you do that?!" I shouted, but I couldn't bring myself to be upset at her. For one, I was too emotionally spent to gather the energy to even feign anger, much less actually be angry. And secondly, in my heart of hearts, I knew that Legend deserved to know.

"I did it for the same reason that you wanna do it! You know it's foul as fuck to hide this from him! You need him to help you through it, and he needs to know what's going on with the woman who agreed to be his wife. It's selfish of your ass to stop him from being the man he wants to be for you!"

Cush yelled right back at me, giving me the tough love that I needed. It was all she had in her to give…growing up the way she did, surrounded by a group of goons for brothers, I was sure it was all she was given, but it was exactly what I needed.

"I'm tired of this fuckin' so-called selfless act you're doing. Not tellin' Legend isn't protecting him. How the fuck you expect him to deal with something he never saw coming? Tell him everything and he'll take it from there. You need to be his woman and let my brother be a fuckin' man. Damn, I'm tired of having to school y'all muthafuckas!" Cush huffed and then crossed her arms in front of her chest as her frown deepened on her face.

Looking at her, I couldn't help but start to laugh. She was a mirror image of her brother, in looks and personality. Here I was going through some real shit, but she'd managed to make me the villain and cuss me out for trying to protect the man I loved. Still, I had to admit that she wasn't wrong.

"You're right," I said, but she just looked at me and shrugged without acknowledging the fact that I'd waved the white flag.

That was Murk's personality shining through. Hearing someone admit that he was right never moved him because, in his mind, he knew he was right and you were just slow as hell for finally seeing it. Cush was the same way. She was a perfect mixture of her bull-headed brothers. I even saw Dame and Quan in her from time-to-time, whenever she started to clown me for random shit or when she showed her emotional side. She was the Dumas girl, a mixture of them all, and I could see why none of her brothers could do a thing with her ass.

Smiling, I was about to lighten the mood with a joke about how she was just as stubborn as her damn brother, but stopped when I heard someone knocking at the door. No...knocking was putting it lightly. Someone was at the door trying to break the damn thing down. It didn't take long before I knew exactly who it was.

"Neesy! Open up this damn door!" Legend's voice roared on the other side, instantly lifting me to my feet.

"Legend, calm down! You just started knocking. Damn!" I shouted as I walked to the door and unlocked it. Before I could even open it for him, he did it for himself and rushed in.

"I left my keys in Miami. You good?" he asked me, his eyes washing over my entire body as if looking for anything that didn't seem right.

Nodding my head, I felt my heart swell with love as I stared at him, feeling the strength of his emotions all at one time. He was exactly what I needed.

"I want you to know that...I love you, Neesy," he told me as he wrapped me in his arms and pulled me close. I lifted my head and kissed him deeply on his lips.

"I love you too."

When Legend pulled away, I tugged him towards the house but his feet stayed firmly planted in the doorway. An uneasy expression crossed his face and he teetered from foot-to-foot, making me frown. He needed to tell me something but he was struggling.

"What is it?" I asked, dropping my hand to my side.

"I have to tell you something," he started and my heart clenched in my chest.

Oh God...What did you do? I thought to myself as I searched his eyes. There was a trace of guilt there...something that I'd never really seen in him before.

"I was hanging out with Darin and..."

He stopped when I frowned at him saying 'hanging out with Darin'. That already didn't sound right.

Seeing the confusion on my face, he cleared his throat and further clarified.

"Actually, I wasn't hangin' with him. His ass dropped by askin' me for advice on some shit with him and Tan. I was kicking him out when...someone knocked on the door. When I opened it, there was a kid there and a bag. Her mother left her with me...said she was mine but she isn't, I swear. Neesy, you gotta believe me...she's not mine."

Totally stunned into silence, I gawked at Legend with my eyes and mouth wide. He continued to stare right back at me, fidgeting with his hands as he waited for me to respond. Tears came to my eyes, but it wasn't from anger. It was from being overwhelmed by all of the many emotions I'd experienced that day.

"How old...how old is she?" I asked, wondering whether or not I would be trying to fight through cancer as well as deal with evidence proving Legend had cheated on me.

"She's old…four-years-old. I wouldn't cheat on you, Neesy," he answered quickly and it put me somewhat at ease.

"Where is she?" I asked him but before he could answer me, I side-stepped him and walked to his rental car, which I'd just noticed was still running.

When I peeked in the back seat, I saw the most beautiful little girl sitting there with a scowl on her face as she glared back up at me, obviously not all that excited about being left in the car by herself. The thick, knotted up brows that she had on her forehead, along with the way her eyes glared beams into me marked her as a true Dumas.

Legend thought she wasn't his…I could see that he genuinely felt that way. But he was wrong. This baby had not only his resemblance, but a little of his brothers as well. And I could tell from the way she glared at me with her nose high in the air that she had the personality to match.

"What's your name?" I asked after pulling the door open.

Pressing her lips together, she looked over at Legend before speaking. He gave her a small nod and then she turned back to me.

"Princess Elsa!" she announced with a smile.

"Um…for real?" I asked, glancing at Legend.

He shrugged and smirked a little as his eyes dropped to meet hers. My heart dropped when I looked at him. As much as he proclaimed this child wasn't his, I could see how much he loved her already; it was written all over his face. His mouth said one thing but his heart said another.

"She doesn't like her real name so I told her she could change it. I mean…who am I to judge when it comes to someone wanting to change her name?" he asked as he scooped her out of the car. "Right, Elsa?"

She immediately dropped her head and laid it against his shoulders, as she wrapped her tiny arms around his neck. He carried her inside and I reached in and grabbed her bag before closing the car door. I needed time to process all of this but, first, we needed to find out if she was really his or not. Although she looked like him, I needed to know for sure so I would know how I needed to react.

Cush, however, didn't see it that way.

"Who is this?!" she asked as soon as we all walked into the house together.

Cush looked from Elsa to Legend and then back again to Elsa.

"Oh shit…" she muttered as she continued to glance between the two, obviously figuring it out on her own. "Legend, tell me you did *not!*"

"I didn't!" Legend replied with his hands out. "I keep tellin' everybody that she ain't mine! I don't even know who her damn mama is, but I swear I'm too much of a pro when it comes to dealin' with hoes for this shit to be happenin'. Not on my damn watch."

"Well, is somebody gonna tell me why she looks like you?" Cush pressed further, as Elsa started walking around the house, examining everything. In her hand was the ugliest little doll I'd ever seen, but she clutched it tightly and spoke to it as she toddled through the house.

"Shiiiiiid…beats me. I just know she isn't mine and I'mma find out who she belongs to as soon as I get a blood test done. But, until then, I'm stuck with her lil' ass," he replied, scratching his head.

Cloaked in silence and stunned by our disbelief, Cush and I watched Elsa as she walked around by herself before hopping into the seat I'd been sitting in at the dining room table. Picking up my fork, she started to poke at the food and scoop it into her mouth.

"Well, at least somebody is eating the food I made," Cush muttered, shooting a look in my direction. "Y'all got a lot to talk about so I'm out. Call me if you need me."

Walking over, Cush hugged me extra tight, probably knowing that I needed it. Then she walked over to Legend and gave him a threatening look, although she didn't say a thing, before walking out the door and shutting it behind her.

"She's not mine," Legend repeated, and I got the odd feeling that he was trying to convince himself and not me.

"Well, in the case that she *is*," I started, keeping my eyes on Elsa, "I'm going to get to know her. She could be a wonderful distraction from everything I got going on."

"You're goin' to be fine, baby," Legend replied, quickly. "I know you and I knew you were flipping the fuck out, trying to deal with this by yourself. But I know it's going to be fine and that's why I'm here."

He scooped me into his arms and kissed me deeply, pressing his lips firmly into mine as he slid his hands over my ass. I stopped him right when he tried to push his hands inside of my pants.

"Stop!" I giggled as I knocked his hand away. "She's right there!"

"Her greedy ass ain't paying attention!" Legend whispered back.

He picked me up and carried me into the large pantry near the kitchen. Before I could protest, he'd already kneeled down and pulled my pants down to the floor. I gasped when I felt his tongue pushing inside of me, roaming over my most sensitive parts.

Reaching out, I gripped the shelves hard, not caring if I pulled the shit down as he kissed, licked and sucked on my nub, bringing me straight to ecstasy.

"Oh God…" I panted.

"Common mistake," he mumbled as he continued to suck. "But I ain't Him."

"Shut up!" I giggled and then moaned again when he pushed his mouth further into me. When he pulled away, his face was covered with my juices and I could barely breathe. Before I could get it together, he'd already released himself and was lifting me up, right above his pole.

"Damn…" he whispered as he began to push in.

The feeling of him entering into inside of me rendered me speechless, as my heart swelled with love and my body leaked from lust.

"I love you," he said against my neck as he held me in place, pushing inside of me carefully. I tried to say it back but my pure, raw emotion swallowed my words. Still, I knew he felt them.

By the time we'd finished and I'd cleaned myself up in our bathroom, I came back down to see Legend and Elsa arguing about what to watch on TV.

"No!" the little girl screamed as she stood in front of Legend with her hands on her tiny hips. "I don't wanna watch dat! I wanna watch *Frozen*!"

"We don't have that bullshit movie here so you gone either have to use your imagination or watch what I'm watchin'!" Legend argued back at her as he sat on the floor, making them eye-level.

As I sat at the entrance of the hallway watching them, I couldn't help but shake my head and laugh quietly. He'd finally met the only woman who could really give him a run for his money. Princess Elsa was not backing down…it didn't matter what Legend said.

"Sit ya lil' bossy ass down. We finna watch *Scarface*. You need to know how the world is for people like us! Them damn Disney movies ain't teachin' you shit about life!"

"Legend, she don't need to know about life yet! She's a kid!" I told him as I walked in, still laughing at the image of them going back and forth about what to watch on TV. She was a handful and a half.

"We'll watch *Frozen* together…Legend, you can go watch *Scarface* in the other room," I told him. "I don't have the movie, Elsa, but I think I can order it."

I reached out for the remote and Legend continued to glare at Elsa as he placed it in my hand.

"Leave it to y'all to gang up on a nigga," he muttered as he turned to me, but I could see the smirk rising up on the side of his face. "Don't think that's how this shit is going to happen for the rest of our lives."

Lifting one eyebrow, I stared at him, not missing a beat.

"The rest of our lives? Oh, I thought you said she wasn't yours?" I reminded him with a sly smile.

He froze, absolutely caught off guard by his mistaken admission of his inner feelings. As much as he denied it, he'd already accepted that Elsa was his.

"She isn't," he said finally, shrugging his shoulders.

"Uh huh," I replied with my smile still intact as I searched for *Frozen* so that we could watch it.

Sitting down next to Legend, who had apparently decided to stay and watch the movie with us, I laid my head on his shoulder and he reached 'round to cup me in his arms. Elsa, happy that she'd gotten her way, came in between the middle of us and plopped her butt right down, snuggling up in between our bodies and making herself comfortable.

And that's how we stayed until the movie was done. Silently wrapped in each other, enjoying each other's presence and the sound of Elsa's laughter. Our little family.

Chapter Twenty

MALIAH

My breathing slowed to nearly a halt as I pulled in front of Danny's apartment. I was surprised by the fact that he lived in a decent community. His spot wasn't big but it was nice and the neighborhood seemed rather quiet. He definitely wasn't in the hood, and I knew that if he was keeping up with the rent in this place, he couldn't be doping up anymore.

"Is this daddy's house?" Shadaej asked, popping her head up to look out the window.

"Mm hmm," I replied, staring at her through the rearview mirror.

"I can't wait to see daddy and show him my cartwheel. I fell last time I showed him but I won't this time!" LeDejah announced, punching her fist into her hand as she spoke. "I'mma nail it!"

Smiling, I stared at her, knowing that she got that phrase from Murk. He was also the one who taught her how to complete a cartwheel. I wondered what Danny would feel about that.

"Okay, let's go. Sha, unbuckle Jari for me?" I asked and she nodded her head.

Letting out a deep breath, I stepped out of the car the same time that Danny's door opened. When I glanced up at him, I couldn't help but admit that he looked damn good. He appeared healthy and sexy as hell, wearing a pair of sweatpants and a wife-beater that showed off his chiseled physique. Sleeping with nasty ass Alicia might have been the best thing to happen to him, because he looked just like the old Danny. He hadn't been using for quite some time.

"Hey, shawty," he said as he came up behind me, his low baritone sending chills down my spine, reminding me about how he used to make my knees weak back in the day.

"Hey, D," I replied back as I grabbed DeJarion in my arms and turned, using him as a buffer between us. He squealed and reached out for Danny, leaping right out of my arms.

"Hey, lil' man," Danny laughed as he held him tightly in his arms, showing off his ripped biceps and triceps.

I shook my head to stop myself from fantasizing and turned back towards the girls who had hopped out of the car.

"Daddddyyyyyyy!" they both yelled.

"We missed you!" Shadaej said as she clamped her arms around her father's legs, giving him a tight hug.

"I missed y'all too, princess," he replied.

He knelt down and gave both of the girls a kiss on the forehead before standing back up and looking at me directly in my eyes. The butterflies returned to my stomach with a vengeance, reminding me of that little piece of my heart that Danny would always have.

"Why don't you come in for a second? Maybe if you see the spot, it'll make you comfortable about leaving the kids with me," his mouth said as his eyes casually glanced over my body.

Even while holding another man's babies in my protruding belly, he gave me a look of pure love, as if I was the only woman that he could ever look at that way. Shaking my head, I cleared my throat and focused on the reason I was there.

"Yes, I would like that," I admitted, following him towards the apartment.

"I know it," he replied with a light chuckle. "I already know your ass was going insane about having the kids with me for the whole weekend. I think you'll like what you see."

Nodding my head, I didn't ignore the fact that Danny was proving that he knew me better than any man probably did. And that included Murk. Danny and I had grown up together and loved each other. But Murk was my husband and the man who never once hesitated to make it real with me.

Danny pumped three babies in me and marriage was never a thought, but Murk didn't think twice about making it official. That was only one situation that showed how much of a man he was about how he did shit. So no matter how much that little piece of my heart that beat for Danny was throbbing in my chest, I knew I'd made the right choice when it came to my life.

*****

"You gotta admit...my shit is laid, ain't it?" Danny asked with a smile on his face that told me he already knew what my answer would be.

"It's a'ight," I joked as I walked to the door. But he was right, his place was nice as hell. I was impressed by how much Danny was able to accomplish and in such a short amount of time. If he was still using, he was hiding that shit good, because there wasn't a trace of anything in the apartment. His spot was furnished and decorated nicely, despite Danny not helping me at all when it came to getting our place together. He'd come a long way.

"I love y'all," I shouted to the kids on my way out. "Be good for Daddy!"

"I love you, too!" they chorused, even DeJarion, but their eyes stayed glued to the TV.

"Aye, can I holla at you for a minute?" Danny asked me and I nodded my head 'yes'.

We walked outside of the apartment and I turned to look at him, waiting for what it was that he needed to say. Danny sighed and ran one hand over the top of his perfectly cut hair, before running his hand over his goatee. His eyes stared so deeply into mine that I began to feel uncomfortable and looked away. My mind wondered if he could sense the discomfort I felt in his presence, but I was sure he could. Danny knew everything about me.

"I just wanted to apologize to you again for all the bullshit we've gone through," he started. Then he grabbed my left hand and fingered the wedding band on my ring finger.

"I know it's too late for us, but I love my kids and I just want to do what's right by them. They have a father who is ready to work towards being in their lives."

I was just about to answer when I heard a gun cock, which made me nearly jump a foot into the air.

"You wanna let go of that hand, muthafucka?" Murk's icy voice said from beside me.

Danny and I had been so focused on each other that he'd walked right up on us without either one of us noticing.

"Murk!" I gasped as I turned to him and snatched my hand away from Danny.

Murk was standing, glaring directly into Danny's face with his gun out and to his side, pointed to the ground.

"The only reason I'm not pointing this at your bitch ass is because the kids are inside. But you touch my fuckin' wife again and I'll body you, nigga. Ya dig?"

You could cut the tension in the air with a dull knife. My eyes swooped over to where Danny was and saw him puff out his chest and bite down on his back teeth, while peering into Murk's face. What I failed to see in Danny's expression was a single shred of fear. And that's how I knew this was about to get bad. Fast.

"Murk, let's just—"

"Get the fuck off my fuckin' property, nigga!" Danny bellowed.

He took a step forward and my heart dropped. I couldn't let this happen. For one, the kids were inside. And secondly, we all had to deal with each other for the rest of our lives…or until DeJarion turned eighteen, so they needed to get it together.

"Y'all can't do this!" I yelled out. "Please, the kids—"

"Fuck nigga, you keep rappin' slick and I'll give you another taste of this fuckin' metal. You must've liked how that bullet felt the first time?"

A spurt of evil laughter escaped Murk's lips as Danny squeezed his fists at his side. I was losing control of the situation.

"Murk—"

But the next series of events happened before I could finish begging Murk to leave peacefully with me. Danny took a step forward and, before he could even get the next word out of his mouth, Murk pulled his hand back and backhanded him hard, while still holding the gun.

"Oh God!" I yelled out as Danny stumbled backwards, holding his face. Blood started to ooze from his lips but he spit it out into the dirt, as he continued to glower at Murk.

"Murk, please…" I pled, holding his arm, but Murk only shook me loose as he stepped in closer to Danny, whose eyes darted quickly down to the gun that Murk was still holding before they lifted back up to his face.

"Keep your hands off my fuckin' wife. I don't want to have to remind yo' ass why the fuck they call me Murk," he threatened before wrapping his arm around my waist.

Danny didn't back down but didn't say a word, either. He was the one in the wrong and he knew it, so there wasn't anything he could say.

Murk had made it clear that he couldn't do shit when it came to the kids, but he definitely could intervene when it came to me. And he was right. I was his wife now and Danny had to respect that.

"Go lick ya wounds, muthafucka," Murk snickered before pulling me away.

I gave Danny one last apologetic glance before turning around to follow Murk to my car. I couldn't say anything at the moment because I was frustrated but also scared. I wondered if Murk could sense how I had been feeling when I was speaking with Danny.

"Go home," he muttered after opening the car door so I could slide in.

And with that, he closed it without giving me a kiss or saying another word. That alone let me know that he knew how to read me even better than I may have initially suspected.

He knows, I thought to myself as I turned on my car and backed out of the parking space. Murk had already jumped in his ride and tore off down the road before I could even shift gears.

He knows that I was feelin' some type of way about Danny.

My heart throbbed in my chest as I tried to hold back the tears in my eyes, knowing that I'd once again hurt the man I loved.

*****

I was alone in the house and it was about 5 am before I heard Murk come home. My mind was racing with all kinds of thoughts of what he could have been up to, of course, including him being with another woman.

"You want to end this?" his voice pierced through the dark, as I lay in the bed clutching on to a pillow and wishing it was him.

"No," I answered quickly, feeling my heart clench tight. It hurt me to the core for him to even feel he needed to ask me something like that.

"Tell me the truth, Li. I gave you a pass when it came to that nigga before, but that's all I got in me. You do that shit again and it's gonna be curtains for him and you. I put that on God," he told me, and I knew without a shadow of a doubt that he was speaking the truth.

Flipping around in the bed, I peered at him through the dimly lit room and shook my head once again.

"I don't want to end this, Murk. I love you and that's all I can say about that. Danny and I have known each other for a long time and…no matter what, I can't bring myself to hate him. But I don't love him anymore. I love you and I'm with you…he's just the father to my kids. And that's all," I concluded with all sincerity and hoped that he understood that what I was saying was the truth.

Murk didn't readily respond, but he did start to take off his clothes before lying in the bed. I wanted to ask him where he'd been but I didn't. I just kept quiet and let my mind think, as he wrapped his arms around me.

"I was at my old condo," he offered as if he already knew where my mind was going. "Alone. I was at my old place, just taking a minute to think about things before I came back here. Another bitch is the last thing you ever have to worry about."

I let out a breath of relief and melted into his arms.

"And another nigga is the last thing you ever have to worry about," I affirmed right back at him.

He nestled his face into my neck and before long, we were both asleep.

Chapter Twenty-One

SHANECIA

"Positive…" I repeated waiting for the tears to come to my eyes. But they didn't come. I was all cried out and I couldn't muster up one if I tried my hardest.

"I have breast cancer."

"You have stage one breast cancer…which means that treatment is possible and you'll make a full recovery so you can put this all behind you. It's noninvasive and we have no indication that it's spread to the lymph nodes. We can fix this, but we have to act fast," Dr. Mitchell told me with a pleasant and hopeful look on his face.

"How soon can we get the surgery scheduled?" Legend asked with a calm tone, as was his nature. That was one of the things that I loved about him. When my mind was roaring, he was calm and able to problem-solve.

"We can get it scheduled as soon as this week. I just have to—"

"Well, let's schedule it. We're ready to get this behind us so we can move the hell on with our lives," Legend interrupted. My eyes fell on him as he held a sleeping Elsa in his lap. She was the prettiest thing I'd ever seen and I wished that she was awake so she could say something that would make me laugh. It was something she'd proven she was good at doing the past few days.

"Okay, let me get some details together and go over a few things. I'll be back in a few," Dr. Mitchell said to us both before walking out the door.

"You good, bae?" Legend asked me, but I didn't need to answer him. His eyes probed mine with understanding of every emotion that I felt inside.

"We can beat this and we will," he added.

"I know," I nodded my head with surety. The entire time he'd been with me, he'd urged me to be positive and I was.

"When we get home, we're going to pack up and jump on a plane. I want to take you somewhere and, I know you have schoolwork and shit to do, but I won't take no for an answer," he informed me with a smile.

"I wasn't going to say no, anyways," I admitted. "I can't wait to go."

*****

"Oh my God…Legend, this is beautiful," I gushed as we walked around the hotel room that he'd reserved for us.

We were definitely in the penthouse of Caesar's Palace in Vegas, the last place I'd thought that Legend would take me, but I was excited. The room was more than I could have even imagined. Everything was trimmed in gold. I felt like a Queen.

"It's less than you deserve, but I can't give you the world just yet," he joked and then kissed me on my lips.

I wrapped my arms around him and deepened our embrace.

"Well, why do I feel like you already have?" I asked and he smiled, instantly warming my heart to see him so happy.

"Where I gonna sleep?" Elsa asked with a confused pout on her face as she cradled her doll, whom she told me was named 'Amber Rozay', a name I was sure she'd gotten from her mother.

"Somebody is coming for you, shorty," Legend said right before someone knocked on the door. "And that's probably them right there."

I watched as Legend walked over to the door and peeked out the peephole. A big smile crossed his face as he stepped back and opened the door. Once I saw who it was outside, I grinned just as wide as he did.

"Maliah!!" I yelled out as I ran and grabbed my cousin in my arms, hugging her about as much as I could with her bulging belly in between us.

"Hey, Murk!" I greeted my future brother-in-law. He leaned over and gave me a hug, lightly kissing the top of my head.

"Hey sis, how you doin'?" he asked as his eyes examined me the same way that Legend had when he first saw me after getting the news. I'd began to get used to certain things the Dumas brothers did, and this was one of them. They leaned more on their own assessment of a situation than what someone told them, and they scrutinized everything.

"I'm good. Legend has been taking good care of me," I told him and he nodded his head, although he already knew it.

Seconds later, the door opened up again and this time, it was Quan and Dame along with their leading ladies, Natoria and Trell, right beside them.

"Bust this shit up! The guests of honor have arrived," Quan announced, wrapping his arm around Natoria.

"Y'all ain't the muthafuckin' guests of honor, I am!" Tanecia said as she ducked in the room from behind them. She walked over and gave me a tight hug and a kiss on the cheek before pulling away. From the look on her face, I could tell that Legend had already told them all the news and they were here to support me.

By this time, I had tears in my eyes as everyone laughed and joked with each other. The hotel staff came in with trays of food, so we all made plates and got to eating. Tanecia took Elsa to go get their nails done, and then the real party began. Murk and Legend lit blunts and Quan made drinks. Dame turned into the DJ and the festivities began.

"Don't drink too much," Legend whispered in my ear as he came up behind me and wrapped his arms around my waist. He bit down softly on my earlobe before kissing me on the cheek.

"Why not? It's a party, right?"

"It's a pre-wedding party," he clarified, making me gasp. "I'm making you my wife tomorrow and I don't need you walking down the aisle with red, drunk eyes."

With my hands over my mouth, I turned to look at him with tears clouding my vision. Leave it to Legend to just up and decide our wedding date and destination for himself. But, to be honest, I really didn't care. I just wanted him and I'm sure he knew that. I didn't care about any of the details…as long as I would be able to be called Mrs. Dumas, I was good to go.

"I invited your mama too, but she said she wouldn't come unless you said specifically it was okay for her to be here. I have a jet waiting to bring her, if you're with it," he offered and I nodded my head slowly.

"I'm with it. She can come."

Smiling, Legend kissed me on my lips and then ran his hands over his goatee as he backed away.

"I gotta talk to my nigga about something," he said, looking at Murk, who caught his stare and ducked his head in acknowledgement. "You chill and have fun. This is your last night as a single woman."

"In that case, I can't wait until it's over."

LEGEND

I was trying my hardest to be strong for Shanecia, but I felt like my armor was failing me. Every time I looked at her, the thought crossed my mind, *how could I make it through this life without her?*

The crazy thing about being in love with someone was that, once they entered your life, they completed you and you weren't whole without them. I couldn't even get used to her not being by my side every night while we were trying the long-distance shit. How was I going to deal with the fact that she could possibly die?

"You need some of this Loud in your life," Murk said as he handed me over a freshly rolled blunt.

Nodding, I took it from his hands and tried to take a pull from it but I couldn't. We were sitting on the roof of the hotel, enjoying an expansive view of the city. It was a sight that people would've paid good money for. But my mind wasn't in it.

"This shit is fuckin' me up inside, Murk. As much as I try to ignore it, it's a real possibility that some shit I can't handle may go down with Neesy. The fuck am I gonna do without her?" I asked, speaking more to myself than to Murk. "How the fuck can I possibly—"

Tears came to my eyes, surprising the fuck out of me and I stopped talking. Just the thought of Shanecia being taken away from me because of the cancer in her body, tore me up inside. She was my reason for breathing and I didn't want to live if I had to do it without her beside me.

"You won't have to," Murk told me as he took the blunt from me and placed it between his lips. "Neesy is a fuckin' survivor and so are you. God ain't bringin' y'all to this shit to fold. It's gonna be fine."

Nodding my head, I took a long swig of Hennessy Black from my glass and enjoyed the burn all the way down. Before I could open my mouth to reply, I heard a stir from behind me. Absentmindedly, I went to grab my piece but stopped when I saw Murk was just chilling and puffin' on his blunt. Obviously, he'd invited company.

"What up, bro?" Quan piped up, as he and Dame walked up on us and sat down on either side of me and Murk.

"We came to make sure you were ready for your wedding day," Dame added.

"Been ready," I replied back with a smirk on my face. "I've been ready for this moment...longer than I even knew."

"Who would've thought this would be you, huh, Leith?" Quan chuckled. "You a family man, just like Pablo over here. Both of y'all got shorties and wives."

Laughing, I didn't even correct him about calling Elsa my shorty. I still had my doubts, but I was getting used to her lil' bossy ass. If she wasn't mine it didn't matter, because I'd kill a muthafucka over her in a second. She was just that important to me and had definitely grown on me. And I loved her regardless to what a blood test may prove.

"Let me pour y'all a shot," Dame said all of a sudden as he pulled out four shot glasses and a bottle of Louis XIII. "You gone bring in the beginning of this marriage the right way...drunk as fuck."

Laughing, I grabbed my shot glass and clinked it with Murk,

Dame and Quan's before draining it in one gulp. My eyes stung but it went down smooth.

"That's some good shit," I told Dame as I glanced at the bottom and he went to pour me another shot.

"For three stacks a bottle, it fuckin' better be," he muttered as he refilled the other shot glasses.

"To my nigga, muthafuckin' Leith Dumas," Murk started with the toast. "May you have many, many years of marital bliss, my nigga."

We tapped our glasses together and took another shot. My brothers all started to talk and laugh about random shit, but I just stared out at the city. Shanecia was heavy on my mind.

God, if you save her for me…I swear, I'll give the dope game up for good, I silently prayed.

And I meant every word.

Chapter Twenty-Two

TANECIA

After talking to Shanecia in Vegas, I finally knew what I wanted to do with my life. The problem was getting everyone else to believe in me enough so that I could do it.

"Your application for a loan was denied," the banker told me with a sympathetic look on her toffee-colored face. "You haven't established any credit history, you don't have a job, no money to put towards the loan…"

"If I had enough money sitting around to put down what you all are asking for, I wouldn't need the damn loan!" I grumbled, narrowing my eyes at the woman. She simply shrugged and pulled her lips into a thin line.

"I don't know what else to tell you," she replied.

"Ugh!" I scowled as I snatched my purse out and ran out of the bank with tears running down my face.

Ever since coming back from Vegas, I had it in my mind that the perfect thing for me to do would be to start up a salon. Shanecia had told me that I needed to start from the bottom and work in someone else's, but my dreams were too big to start from the bottom. I wanted to go big time and own my own spot so I could hire stylists to work in it with me. To be honest, I only knew how to do a few styles on my own so I wouldn't make it if I worked in anyone else's place. I needed to be the boss.

"Where you been?" Darin asked as soon as I walked in the house.

"Out," I replied back in a dry tone.

Things weren't any better between us. Although I could tell he was trying to get it right with me, the more I thought about what happened between us and our argument at the cookout, the angrier I became. Darin was just like any other man I'd encountered…he was just a lot politer. But, at the end of the day, he was still only ready for a relationship with me if he could call the shots and do the things how he wanted. I wasn't for that so I needed to get my own shit so I could get out.

"Tan, how many times do I have to tell you that I'm sorry?" he asked as he walked over to where I was standing in the kitchen with the refrigerator open.

"Until I believe it…or, better yet, you don't have to tell me shit!" I said with a shrug and then flinched when I saw he had Jen in his arms. I thought about what Shanecia had said about her hearing me curse and repeating it. I didn't want that to happen.

"Jen and I miss you," he said, holding her up like a puppet as he spoke.

"No, *you* miss me because you need someone to do all the things for her that I used to…you know, back then when I was under the impression that I could love her like my own daughter. Back then before I realized you just saw me as her nanny."

I knew my words were cutting Darin to the core, but I was still hurt and I wanted him to feel the way that I did when he constantly threw in my face about how Jen was *his* daughter and *he* knew best when it came to her. I'd been punishing him for days over what happened, but I still didn't feel like he understood it.

Just as I was about to walk into the guestroom where I'd been sleeping, Darin walked up behind me and grabbed my arm, pulling me around so that I was looking directly in his face.

"Listen and listen good because I'm only gone say this shit once," he began, shocking the shit out of me with his tone. He paused and I wasn't sure if I should respond or not. In truth, I was stunned into disbelief at Darin's new and improved thug persona and I didn't know what to say.

"I—I'm listening," I replied back finally.

"When I told you I loved you, I fuckin' meant that shit! You ain't goin' no muthafuckin' where and neither am I, so get out yo' fuckin' feelings so we can move on with our lives. I ain't gone stand by and let you move around in the streets like you ain't got no nigga, so get yo' mind right before I get it right for you. Ya dig?"

He ended his statement with a piercing stare that made a lightbulb go off in my head. I squinted my eyes at him and scrutinized his stance. Something seemed oddly familiar about it.

"You been talkin' to Legend, huh?" I asked with a smile.

Darin gave me a blank look as if he was going to deny it and then his shoulders dropped and he nodded his head.

"Yeah… I been going to him for advice and he told me what I should do. I didn't want to say all that shit but I was desperate! You can't keep acting like this, Tan! I love you and I want us to work. I've always loved you," he told me with his shoulders hunched over in defeat.

Giggling, I shook my head. I couldn't get over the fact that he'd actually gone to Legend to get some advice about our situation. That was definitely a desperate move. Legend was probably the last person on Earth to get relationship advice from. Maybe Darin really did care.

"Maybe we can go out to dinner and talk about it…" I said slowly.

My smile grew on my face when Darin looked up with a hopeful look in his eyes. It was so damn cute.

"You swear?"

"Yes…we can," I answered with a sigh. "Truth is, I've missed you too, Darin. I just don't like how you made me feel when it came to Jen. I love her just like I would if she was mine. Isn't that what you would want out of a woman who you're dating? To love your kid like Jen's hers?"

Darin nodded his head while pondering my words. "Yes, you're right. Can we just put this all behind us and start over?"

I thought it for a minute but it didn't take long for me to come up with my answer. When I heard the news about Shanecia's cancer, it tore me up inside to think of what my sister was going through. But it also let me know that life could change in a blink of an eye. We didn't have time to sit around and be mad about little shit when it came to people we loved…because they could be taken away at any time. In my heart, I knew Shanecia would be fine but her situation still made me realize a lot of things.

"Yes, we can," I told him with a smile. Then I walked forward and wrapped my arms around his neck.

"I love you, Darin," I whispered in his ear.

"I love you, too," he replied. "And since I do…I have a surprise for you."

When I pulled away from Darin, he reached in his pocket and pulled out a check. I looked at it and a grin crossed my face as tears clouded my eyes.

"What's this?" I asked him as I rubbed the tears away.

"I know you've been trying to get this salon shit together and been having issues…I heard you on the phone," he explained when he saw the confusion in my eyes. "I just want to invest in your dream… to invest in you. I know you can do it; you just need your man's help."

Jumping into Darin's arms, I covered his face with kisses.

"Thank you so much, baby," I said through the tears that were falling down my cheeks. "I won't let you down. I promise."

"I won't let you down either."

Chapter Twenty-Three

SHANECIA

"I'll be right here when you get out," Legend told me as I stared into his eyes, enjoying the comfort in his gape. There was nothing but pure love there and it was the last thing I would think about before the surgery.

But when the anesthesia started to put me under, the only thing I could think about was the most important day of my life: the day in Vegas when I finally became Mrs. Dumas.

The weather was terrible. It was raining cats and dogs and 'some more shit' according to Legend. But not even that could dampen my mood.

"You sure you ready for this?" Maliah asked, as she walked in dressed like a goddess in a long flowing purple dress that celebrated her bodacious figure and growing belly in just the way I'd thought it would when we picked it out.

Although I was getting married in Vegas, I didn't want to half-ass my day. Legend and I had found a beautiful chapel that looked like it had been built centuries before, but had been updated while keeping intact all of the regal splendor that its patrons adored. When we passed it, I couldn't keep my eyes off of it and Legend told me that no matter what he had to do, I would be getting married inside of it. True to his style, he made it happen. I didn't think for one second that he couldn't.

"I'm more than ready," I told her and watched as she gasped and put her hand to her mouth when her eyes fell on me.

I was in the most beautiful dress that I'd ever laid eyes on and felt just as beautiful as Legend made me feel every day. My stomach had jitters but it wasn't because of the vows I would take…I was anxious to know if Legend would love the dress as much as I did. I just wanted to please him…I wanted to make him feel the way he made me feel every day. I didn't know what our future lives would turn into, but I wanted him to remember this day, this moment, for the rest of his life.

"Can I let everyone else in? They are about to have a cow waiting for you to let them see the dress," Maliah said with a giggle, as she smoothed her hair back before running a hand over her belly.

Nodding, I tried to bite down the smile that teased my face as I stared at myself in the floor-length mirror. I wasn't wearing a custom-made gown because we were doing everything so fast, but it couldn't get any better if I had designed it myself. It was a long, white, silk gown, covered in Swarovski crystals. The train trailed behind me and the crystals sparkled in the light in a way that would certainly catch every eye in the room, although I was only worried about one pair of eyes.

"Neesy! You are gorgeous!" Tanecia squealed as she entered the room, holding Elsa's hand.

"Ohhhh!" Elsa added from right beside her and then ran over to get a better look at my dress. "It's pretty!"

"You're beautiful, Princess Elsa!" I smiled as I looked at her.

She was my flower girl, dressed in a mini version of my own gown, with a crown of flowers around her head. Tanecia had hooked up her hair really quick with a braid and curls design. From the way she did it, she probably needed to go into business as a hairstylist because she did the damn thing on my hair, Maliah's, and Elsa's, as well as her own.

"Did she make it?" I asked, looking at Tanecia with an uneasy look on my face.

"She's here. She just decided to give you your space," she told me with an even tone.

Glancing off to the side, I looked at Maliah but she offered no assistance at all. This one I had to decide on my own. Was I ready to forgive my mother and move on with my life? Had she really changed? Was she really getting better?

"She can come in," I said, finally doing something that I always struggled with: making a decision.

"You sure?" Tanecia asked one last time and I nodded my head.

"She can. It's fine," I replied with a sigh and then turned back to the mirror. "This is a new beginning for all of us."

After the oohs and ahhs were over, we walked out to the fleet of cars that Legend had reserved to take us to the wedding. The car sitting at the head of the group was an all-white Maybach with golden leather interior inside. The chauffeur was standing outside with a sign that read 'Bride' *and it put a smile on my face. It was beautiful.*

"Mama," I said, calling out to her. "Can you ride in the car with me?"

Her eyes grew wide with surprise, and she nodded her head. I held out my hand to grab hers and laced our fingers together. It surprised me how my heart pinged in my chest when she tightened her grip on my hand. Right then, I realized how much I really needed my mama.

"Neesy, you really look beautiful," she said once we sat down in the back of the Maybach. I looked at her and saw that her eyes were misty with tears which made mine cloud over as well.

She looked so much better than she had the last time I'd seen her. Her skin was clear and her weight was back. She was dressed in a beautiful purple and silver dress, looking just like the perfect Mother of the Bride. Legend had given Tanecia money to find her s dress and pair it with the beautiful jewels that were draped around her neck and wrists. She was breathtaking to see. I felt like I was looking at my mama...the woman I'd grown my whole life loving. It was as if the last year never happened.

"Thank you, Mama," I told her, wiping at my eyes.

"Don't cry, you'll mess up your makeup," she said with a little chuckle as she handed me a tissue.

"Don't worry...Maliah airbrushed this on my face. I don't think it's going anywhere for a very long time. I have no idea how to get it off!" I replied, laughing along with her.

We laughed a little more and then the car went silent, each of us retreating into our own thoughts. Then, just as I was about to say something, she beat me to it.

"Baby, I hope that we can get past everything that's transpired. I love you, Shanecia, and I'm sorry for the woman I became when you left to go to college," she admitted, tears running down her face. I reached out and dabbed at one with the tissue in my hand.

"I just didn't know what to do or how to deal with it after you left. You were all I had...after your father left, I relied on you so much that I didn't know what to do once you left. Tan was there but then...she really wasn't," she paused and chuckled a bit. "You know how Tan is...always so caught up with her own issues, she wasn't thinkin' about little old me. Then I started using and I pushed her even further away..."

Shaking my head, I stopped her from speaking. Then I cleared my throat and grabbed both of her hands in mine.

"This is a happy day...a new beginning, Mama. We are going to put all of that behind us and move forward, okay?" I told her and she nodded her head.

"I love you and I forgive you...but only if you'll forgive me for how I've acted these past few months," I started, sniffling as my eyes clouded with more tears. "You needed me while you were in rehab and I wasn't there for you because I was angry. I'm sorry."

Smiling, Mama nodded her head.

Then she said, "Don't worry...that husband-to-be of yours checked in with me every week and threatened the shit out of me! He made sure to let me know every time he came in that he would fuck my ass up if I didn't get better for you! He loves you, baby."

Smiling, I confirmed her words with a nod of my own.

"I know he does. And I love him, too."

And there, about an hour later, inside of the most beautiful and majestic building I'd ever seen, I said 'I do' to the only man on Earth who could ever deserve my love.

Legend was jaw dropping...absolutely breathtaking...in an all-white suit, with diamond studded ears, a clean cut, and the whitest Jordan sneakers I'd ever seen in life.

You can take the man out the hood but you can't take the hood out the man, I thought as I looked at him, his appearance reminding me of the day I saw him at the gas station. To be honest, that was the day things between us changed. And now here we were...making the vow to love each other to life.

"I now pronounce you husband and wife! You may kiss your bride!"

We were in the church and standing right in front of the altar, but Legend didn't give a damn. He leaned over, gripped my ass in his hands, and kissed me like it was only us standing there. By the time he finished, it felt like he'd given me every damn thing but the dick right then. I was winded, panting and wet as hell. Like Maliah, I made it up in my mind that we would be dipping out of the celebration early so I could make it official with my husband.

"I love you, Neesy," Legend said once he'd broken our kiss. He looked at me like there was no one else in the room. Many pairs of eyes were watching us, waiting for us to walk down the aisle so they could yell and scream, but Legend wasn't worried about any of them.

"I love you, too," I told him. "I promise I do."

"I know it," he replied back with ease, biting down on his bottom lip.

I thought he was about to kiss me again and I felt throbbing between my thighs. I wanted him just as much as he wanted me. Maybe even more.

"They are looking at us," I said finally, feeling a little nervous about the crowd seeing how intensely Legend was staring at me. He made me feel like I was the only woman in the world. And, to him, I was.

"Naw...all eyes are on you," he corrected me. "Because you're so fuckin' beautiful."

"Legend!" I squealed my laughter. "You can't say that in the church."

"With you by my side, I can do whatever the hell I want to do," he replied. Then he reached down and scooped me into his arms, cradling me.

"Ladies and gentleman, I present to you, MY MUTHAFUCKIN' WIFE!" his voice thundered out.

"SALUTE!" his brothers yelled out, each of them holding their guns up in the air.

"Sweet Jesus!" the man who married us yelled out. "They aren't going to shoot those in here are they?"

Legend laughed as he watched the man duck down and scurry to the side of the building.

"You good, man," Legend said, while laughing as he carried me down the aisle in front of our family who was clapping and smiling. "It's Saturday and my niggas don't kill on Saturdays."

"Okay...looks like she's finally just about sleep," I heard Dr. Mitchell say from somewhere above me. "Alright, Shanecia. We'll see you in a little while. Sleep tight."

Chapter Twenty-Four

LEGEND

"She already in?" Murk asked me as he walked into the waiting room where I sat, trying my hardest to keep my mind off the fact that Shanecia was in a room somewhere being cut open.

"Yeah," was all I said while running my hand over the top of my head.

"Nigga, you looked stressed as fuck," Murk told me.

He sat down next to me and looked at my side profile, probably trying to read me, but I wasn't going to give him the satisfaction of knowing I was fucked up inside. I'd just married Shanecia a few days ago and we spent the most perfect of days in Vegas, before going to Los Angeles where I'd rented a house for us to enjoy right on the beach in Malibu.

She radiated perfection every single day. She looked healthy and beautiful...she was the perfect woman. What I couldn't understand was how anything could be wrong with her. She didn't look like she had cancer but that was Shanecia. No matter how she may have felt...how weak or tired or scared...she wouldn't show any of that to me because she didn't want me to worry. What she didn't understand was that as long as I had breath in my body, I would always worry about her.

"I'm good," I replied back. "What your brothers up to?"

"They on the way. Had to set up some shit at the house for you, but we all wanted to be here when she wakes up since the ladies were here before she went in," Murk replied back. "We wanted to give them a break, plus be here for you and Neesy."

"I appreciate y'all."

"Don't mention it," Murk said as soon as my phone started to ring.

Looking down, I felt uneasy when I saw who it was calling. She had the worst damn timing.

"Yeah," I answered the call.

"Legend...I—I'm not calling to bother you or anything like that. But I did want to get you the results of Onika's, I mean Elsa's, DNA test," Agent Martinez said on the other line, using a tone much different from any one that she'd used in the past.

Ever since the incident at the house, I'd shaken her and she'd stayed off our case. She believed me when I told her that Dame, Murk and I didn't kill her friend and, although she was upset that I wouldn't give her any information on who did, she was able to accept the fact that Sarafin had been fuckin' with the streets and the streets fucked her right back. She made her own choice to deal with Mello and, because of it, she lost her life.

"I'm listenin," I responded, my tone not matching the feeling in my chest.

Elsa had begun to grow on me in a way that I'd least expected. That morning when I dropped her off at Tanecia's while I was at the hospital with Shanecia, Elsa called me 'daddy' and, for the first time since I met her, I responded to her, without feeling the need to tell anyone that she wasn't mine. My heart had finally accepted that she was my blood and I didn't know what I would do if she was taken away from me.

"Well...you'll be happy to know that you were right," Martinez told me. "She's not yours."

I sucked in a breath as my chest tightened. My soul was crushed at hearing the words that I'd prayed to hear the day that I first laid eyes on Elsa. Closing my eyes, I sucked in another deep breath and let it out easily, willing myself not to lose my mind.

She wasn't mine. Elsa had a father and it wasn't me. I was going to have to figure out how to let her go.

"But...the thing is she's still related to you," Martinez continued.

"WHAT?!" I said, much louder than I'd expected. "How in the hell...what do you mean she's related to me?"

Murk turned to look at me, unable to hear the call, but my reaction to what Martinez was saying piqued his curiosity and he started to tune in. At that exact moment, Dame and Quan came around the corner laughing about something that they'd been talking about. But what Agent Martinez said next would surely wiped the smiles right off their faces.

"What I mean is…from the DNA, we can tell that you aren't the father but one of your brothers is," she continued. "If they are available to take a test, I'm at the lab now at the hospital you came to for the test. If they can't come in now—"

"They'll be there in five minutes. We're already here," I said and then hung up the phone.

When I ended the call, all three of my brothers were looking at me with serious expressions on their face, waiting for me to fill them in on what was going on.

"That was Agent Martinez—"

"Ah shit, not that bitch," Murk muttered.

"Naw, she called me about Elsa's paternity test," I told them all as they looked at me attentively. "And y'all ain't gone believe this shit."

*****

"Aww, *hell* to the *fuck* naw!" Dame yelled so loud that everyone standing in the hall turned in our direction. "How the fuck am I gonna explain this shit to Trell?!"

Shaking my head, I tried my best to stop a smile from rising up on my face. All of Dame's days of hoeing around the city had finally caught up with him, and this time what I'd always told him finally came true.

"Nigga, how many times I told you to strap up before you catch some shit you can't get rid of?" I reminded him of the warning I'd given him so many times. "Well, now you got something you can't get rid of… a daughter."

"FUCK!" Dame cursed loudly once more, making a petite nurse that was walking by us flinch. "Trell just took me back and I just put that fuckin' ring on her finger a few months ago! She ain't even got comfortable with that shit! She ain't gone have no problem snatching that bitch right off and throwing it at my ass!"

"Calm down, Dame! After all the shit you done put her ass through, you should be happy it's only one kid," Quan reminded him. "You done gave her STDs and shit... pretty much told her ass that you don't give a damn about her life. This should be an easy pill to swallow!"

"Nigga, shut da fuck up!" Dame shot back at Quan. He reached out to grab him but Quan dipped out of the way, laughing his ass off at Dame's expense.

"Hey, at least she ain't ugly!" Murk reasoned, saying the same damn thing I'd told Elsa when I first saw her. "Don't nobody want no ugly muthafuckas dumped on them. That should make the news easier for Trell to deal with."

"True," I added, nodding my head. I wasn't happy that Elsa wasn't mine, but I liked the fact that she would always be in the family. Her being my niece was the next thing to her being my daughter. I could watch her, and then take her ass back to her real daddy whenever she started waving that ugly ass doll around and getting on my nerves about watching *Frozen* all day.

"Ain't none of y'all niggas ever gonna be shit," Dame fumed with a frown on his face. "I hate all y'all. How the fuck I end up with a kid who acts like Leith? Shit!"

"Mama gave me the good genes," I explained to him with a shrug.

"Princess Elsa is destined for greatness."

"Yeah, yeah, yeah, nigga," Dame said. "My first act as daddy is to let you know that y'all won't be callin' her that shit."

"You'd rather Onika?" I asked him with a smirk on my face. Dame's eyes rose to the ceiling as he thought for a minute and then looked back at me.

"Elsa it is," he replied. "Damn it."

"She's a good kid, Dame," I told him with a pat on the back. "I'm gonna miss her."

"Aww, look at Leith actin' all caring and shit," Quan teased. "Don't tell me the little lady broke down your heart of stone when it comes to jits."

Chuckling to myself, I didn't respond as I walked away to check on Shanecia's progress. But what he'd said was true. Elsa had done that and I was going to miss seeing her every day and being the one responsible for her.

But the more I thought about it, I figured that she'd fulfilled her purpose with me. I finally had my heart set on having a child of my own. And as soon as the doctor cleared Shanecia and gave her a clean bill of health, I was gonna put one right up into her ass.

SHANECIA

When I came to, the first face I saw was Legend's. But it felt like a dream. My vision was cloudy and my head felt light. It wasn't until he stood up and touched me lightly on the side of my face that I knew I wasn't dreaming.

"I heard you were a soldier in there…how you feelin'?" he asked me with a low tone, almost as if he were afraid he'd hurt me by speaking above a whisper.

"Tired," I was able to whisper out as I enjoyed the feel of Legend's touch on my face.

"You feel any pain?" he asked me and I shook my head.

"I'm still pretty numb so it's just a dull ache. Other than that, I'm fine."

Looking down, I noticed the bandages wrapped tightly around my chest…where my breasts had been. Immediately, tears came to my eyes. Against everyone's warnings, I'd looked up pictures online to get an idea of the type of scarring I would have so that I could prepare myself mentally. I thought that if I went in knowing what the outcome would be, that I would adjust well to it all. Unfortunately, I was wrong.

A tear escaped and slid down my eye, causing Legend to frown. He wiped it away and I bit my lip, willing myself not to release another when I saw the sadness in his eyes.

"Baby, what's wrong?" he asked, his eyes moving rapidly back and forth as he searched mine.

"Will you still love me...with them gone? Will you still like the way I look? There will be scars and..."

My voice trailed off as tears flooded my eyes when I saw the stricken look on Legend's face. I didn't know whether he was shocked about the scarring that I told him I'd have, or the fact that I was breaking down right in front of his eyes...something I'd never done in front of him before. I'd always prided myself on being so poised and in control in the midst of the most intense and nerve-racking situations. But here I was, absolutely losing it.

"Calm down...Neesy, stop that damn crying. Stop fuckin' wasting your tears over some bogus shit," he told me as he wiped at my face.

I reached over, wincing from the pain that shot through my underarm, and grabbed a handful of Kleenex from the box on the table beside the bed. If he could love me through this ugly cry, he could love me through anything. Snot was bubbling out of my nose and my face was covered with tears that were coming down my face in boatloads. All of the emotions I'd kept at bay for the past few months, were piling in and flushing out of me all at once.

"Of course I'll still love you. I don't care about that superficial shit," Legend said as he kissed me on my lips, in the midst of my tears. "I'm an ass man any way. You know that shit. And you don't even have an ass but I still love your bighead ass anyways, lil' booty girl."

Through the tears, I smiled deeply and almost let out a giggle at his joke. It hurt to laugh and I flinched a bit at the pain, but Legend rubbed the side of my face to calm me down. His touch was the perfect remedy.

"But if it's that important to you to have some breasts, I'll get you the best titties that money can buy. I got bread so I can make it happen…if that's what you want," he added with a straight face.

Blinking, I looked at him trying to figure out if he was serious before bursting out into laughter, which I regretted doing when the pain kicked in.

"You have no damn sense, I swear," I told him, shaking my head from side-to-side as I looked at him.

"Yeah, but you married me so how much sense that give you?" he asked with a smirk on his face as he climbed up into the bed with me.

Breathing deeply, I relaxed in his arms as he cradled my body and kissed my face. Seconds later, I was fast asleep, dreaming, once again, of the day I became his.

Chapter Twenty-Five

SHANECIA

3 months later

"Daaaaamn, Neesy, you think you went big enough?!" Maliah asked me as she walked up to greet me on the sidewalk leading up to the rec center.

Reaching out, I grabbed her into a hug and pulled her close. After we broke our embrace, she stepped back and looked at me, her eyes glued to my chest.

"What you mean?" I asked feeling suddenly self-conscious.

"I mean them tig ole bitties! Got damn yo' bosoms are huge!" she exclaimed while continuing to ogle me. I laughed when she reached out and poked one all carefully as if it would burst if she pressed too hard.

"You can touch them, they won't bite you," I told her with a roll of my eyes.

"Heffa, you done upgraded on these hoes. I love them though. Damn, they look natural and all. Bish, is you wearing a bra?" she asked in a low tone but with a sneaky grin on her face.

"Nope!"

"Aw, hell naw! And them thangs sittin' up like that?! Sign me up for whoever did that so they can do these in a few months. Murk been talkin' about I gotta breast feed and shit. If I know what I think I know, then his greedy ass kids gone be attached to one of my titties all damn day. By the time I wean them off my milk, my shits gone be swooping back and forth on the floor. I'mma need the number to your surgeon ASAP!" Maliah spat out all in one breath.

It seemed to me that her 'swooping breasts' might have been a concern of hers for quite some time from how she threw all that out there with ease.

"Well, Legend told me he was gone buy me the best titties money could buy…his words not mine," I added with a giggle.

"And that's exactly what his ass did. You ready for this walk?" she asked and I nodded my head. "Good. I gotta get these babies out because I can't take this shit no longer. I was up all last night with heartburn. If I gotta do this shit for another week, I'm not gone make it!"

Shaking my head at Maliah's dramatic flair, I picked up my pace so that I could walk along side of her. She had called early that morning and begged me to meet her at the rec center so I could walk around the track with her. According to the call, she needed me there just in case she fell out because she was determined not to leave the track until her contractions were less than a minute apart. From the determined look on her face, she wasn't kidding.

"So what's been going on with Danny? He doing okay with the kids?" I asked her, trying to strike conversation to get my mind off the sun that was beaming down on my head.

"Yeah, he's good with them. I'm still trying to get used to the fact that I don't have them every other weekend but, in all honesty, they like spending time with him and, from what I've seen, he's not doing too bad while he has them," she told me between heavy breaths.

"And how is Murk taking it?" I asked with one brow lifted and a hint of skepticism in my voice. I couldn't see Murk ever coming to terms with the fact that Danny would be a part of Maliah's life, so I knew it had to be hard dealing with that entire situation.

"Murk is Murk, what can I say?" She shrugged and rolled her eyes. "The good thing is they haven't gotten into a fight since that one time that I had to break them up. Murk still drives by Danny's house when he has the kids sometimes. I don't think he'll ever stop that. In Murk's mind, those are his kids too, and he has the right to check in on them."

Laughing, I shook my head. "Well, you can't blame him for that. It's a good thing that he loves them just as much as you do."

Maliah smiled, a sappy expression crossing her face.

"Yes, that he does. And I love him for it."

Nodding, I focused back on the track as Legend came to my mind at that exact moment. I wondered if I should bring up the fact that he and I had spoken about having a baby. After battling it back and forth, I decided to go ahead and say something, but Maliah started to speak before I did.

"How's everything going between you and Alicia?"

I thought on it for a bit before answering. To be honest, we were still rebuilding our relationship but she definitely was trying. According to the therapists at the rehabilitation center, she was progressing just how they'd expected her to, and she was only a couple months out from being released on her own, if she was ready. I was very proud of her on that end, but I just had to build back up to thinking of her in the way I had before dealing with her addiction issues.

"We're good. Just working towards getting things back to how they were," I replied back honestly.

"I know what you mean. My mama is still dipping around with the pastor, but she says he makes her happy so who am I to judge her?" Maliah admonished with a shrug.

"Funny how we swapped places with them, right? We got our lives together and now they are the ones trying to piece theirs together." I laughed as I thought about it. Maliah added her own dry laughter and shook her head.

"If that's what you call what Loretta is doing. She gettin' something but I don't think it's her life."

Sighing, I laughed a little and rolled my eyes at Maliah talking about her mama. Deciding to change the subject, I continued on.

"We had little miss Elsa over last weekend and Mama came over to hang with us. We did our hands and nails. Elsa's was so cute."

"How's Legend doing with her being with Dame now?" Maliah asked me, and I smiled as I thought about Legend's relationship with Elsa.

"Legend is good because he still has her all the damn time. He gave her a cellphone and she calls him every day to tell on Dame, and Legend plays right into it. He'll curse Dame's ass out about that little girl. She loves her Uncle Legend," I told Maliah with a roll of my eyes. "And she's the apple of his eye."

"Anybody heard from Trell?"

I nodded my head. "Yeah, she told me that she just needed a minute to get her mind around Dame having a daughter. I don't blame her...she's been through a lot all because Dame couldn't keep it in his pants. And now she has to figure out if she wants to raise another woman's child. Tan is doing it but not every woman is down with that shit. It's good for Dame, though. He has his hands full dealing with Elsa."

Before I could say another word, a car came in quick and swerved to a halt right alongside the path we were walking, making both of us nearly jump straight out of our skin.

"MALIAH! What da fuck I told you about this shit?!" Murk said as soon as he jumped out of the driver's side and slammed the door closed behind him.

Sniffing with indignation, Maliah threw her hands on her hips and scowled at him.

"I'm tired of sittin' up in that damn bed! I want these twins out!" she yelled at him but he wasn't hearing it.

"I don't give a fuck what you want! The doctor said you needed to lay your ass up in the bed until it was time, and that's exactly what the fuck you gone do! Get in the damn car before you hurt my shorties!"

Murk shot back, without missing a beat.

His eyes shot to me and he dipped his head subtly, giving me a quick greeting before returning his glare to Maliah, who was staring at him defiantly.

"Get your ass in the car, Li!"

"I ain't goin' nowhere! I can do what I want and neither you nor that white ass doctor gone tell me shit!" Maliah roared with her hands on her hips and I couldn't help but laugh at her. "What she know about Black women bodies anyways? Every woman on my mama side walked their babies out, and I'mma do the same thing and walk these muthafuckas ou—AHHH!"

Before she could finish her sentence, Murk had already walked forward and scooped her pregnant self straight up off the ground, and began to carry her to the car. I bent over and grabbed my stomach, laughing uncontrollably as I watched the two of them go back and forth.

"Don't nobody understand them ghetto ass broads from your mama's side of the family, but what I want your ass to understand is you gone sit up in that bed until my lil' niggas come up out of there!"

"Murk, put me doooooown! I swear, I hate you!" Maliah spat back as she tried to fight against him, but Murk only tightened his grip before bending down to stuff her in the car.

She wasn't a match for him and she knew it, no matter how much she tried to fight it. No matter what Maliah said and how she acted, I knew she liked it too. Murk was serious about his little ones...what mother wouldn't want that?

*****

"Bae...wake up," Legend grumbled as he shoved my arm, pulling me out of a deep sleep. "Yo' fuckin' phone ringing and you need to answer that shit. I'm tired as fuck."

Rubbing my eyes, I tried to keep myself from suffocating Legend with my pillow and decided instead to see who it was calling me at this ungodly hour.

"Hello?"

"Neesy...OH SHIT!"

"Huh?" I replied, frowning at the phone. Then I pulled it away to see who it was.

"Maliah?"

"Neesy, these contractions about to split my ass open, I swear. Good Lord...Murk, drive faster, please! Neesy, I'm about to have the babies!"

My heart leaped in my chest and I jumped out of the bed so fast that I pulled the covers right off of Legend.

"Gotdammit, Neesy! I said I'm fuckin' tired!" he grumbled as he sat up to snatch them back, but I batted them out of his hands.

"Legend, Maliah is about to have the babies!" I yelled out and was met by a blank stare.

"Li-Li, Legend," I clarified. "She's about to have the babies! Get out the damn bed!"

"OH SHIT!" he exclaimed as he jumped up and walked to the bathroom. "My nigga 'bout to be a muthafuckin' pops for real!"

Rolling my eyes at Legend, I tuned back into the phone in time to hear Maliah telling one of the hospital workers that she couldn't hold the babies in anymore.

"Ma'am, you have to wait until we—"

"I'm not waitin' for shit!" I heard her yell. "I'm about to spread my legs east and west so I hope one of y'all asses can catch these babies!"

"Well, I guess they made it to the hospital," I snickered and then winced when Maliah yelled out in pain. "Li, we're on our way," I told her after her howls subsided.

"Thank God for you, Neesy, because Murk over here ain't worth shit! All the damn things this nigga done seen and he actin' like he gone puke or some shit!" she said in a way that let me know she was glaring directly at Murk. Then her demands started up yet again.

"Listen, y'all finna see some parts of me ain't nobody in the world ever seen if you don't get me to a fuckin' room soon! And I used to be a stripper, so I done showed people a lot of shit!"

And with that, I gasped and hung up the phone. Maliah was showing out for real. I sent a quick text to her mother to let her know what was going on, just in case she hadn't told her, and started getting ready to get to the hospital.

Part of me was a little sad as I thought about how exciting it would be when my time came to deliver a love baby that me and Legend created. But I shook that part off and immediately became excited for the lives that Maliah was about to bring forth.

I couldn't wait to see the babies.

*****

When we turned down the hall for Maliah's room, the first person I saw was Murk, standing outside and pacing. Immediately, I examined his face and my stomach dropped in my chest as I wondered what had gone wrong. Legend must have been thinking the same thing because he reached out and grabbed my hand as if to calm me down.

"Aye, bro, you good?" Legend asked him.

Murk flinched a little, finally noticing that we had walked up on him, which was uncharacteristic of someone who was always surveying his surroundings. In all the time that I'd known Murk, he had always been so reserved, stealthy and watchful…it seemed nearly impossible to sneak up on him without him knowing you were coming from miles away. But right now, he definitely wasn't himself.

"Legend, my mind is fuckin' spinnin', for real," he started. "I need to light up after the shit that I done seen. When I tell you I done seen some shit but I ain't never seen a muthafuckin' pussy open so gotdamn wide! And the worst part is…ain't no fuckin' unseeing that shit, nigga! Her shit opened big as my head! Fuck…I need to smoke one."

Legend and I both stopped and stared at him, each of us probably thinking the same thing: Murk needed to get the shit smacked out of him right then.

"Nigga, you over here pacing and shit just because…did she have the damn babies or not?" Legend asked him.

Murk wiped some sweat off his brow and then nodded his head.

"Yeah, she just spit them things out of her…you-know-where. Shit, it was so fuckin' nasty, man—"

Rolling my eyes at Murk and his issues coming to terms with the female anatomy, I walked into the room behind him so that I could comfort Maliah, because obviously her baby daddy wasn't doing shit.

"Li-Li!" I said as I walked over to where she was. "Are you okay?! You look so tired."

"Hell yeah, because I am," she replied back just above a whisper. Her hair was sweaty and matted to her head, but she still was able to give me a small smile.

"The babies are over there with Mama. They cleaning them…you see them?" she asked and I turned around but instead of seeing the babies, I was looking right at the chest of a physician.

"Ma'am, you can't be in here without the proper gear on and you need to wash up. Please leave and we will let you know when you can come back in," the doctor promptly informed me.

Glancing back at Maliah, I gave her a look and she shrugged. It looked like that one subtle movement took all the energy from her. Rolling my eyes, I backed away but stopped short to get a peek of the babies before I left. They were still getting washed up but they were the perfect little angels. One boy and one girl.

Not even crying, they were sitting quietly as the nursing staff rubbed them down, wiping away all the blood and goo that came along with their miracle delivery. I could see from where I stood that they both had Maliah's complexion but Murk's hazel eyes. They were adorable.

"Aww," I whispered to myself, a smile creeping up on my face. They looked so calm and reserved although they had just been pushed through from one world to another.

And then, suddenly, I felt my knees go weak and my eyes grow heavy. Something was wrong and I knew it as soon as I started to see the black spots in front of my eyes. I opened my mouth to call out for help, but I was too tired to get a single word out.

"Ma'am, I told you that you can't be in here…Ma'am, are you, okay? Ma'am!"

*****

When I awoke, I was lying in a hospital room, similar to the one Maliah was in, and I was no longer in my own clothes. My heart thumped in my chest as I wondered what had happened. Naturally, the first feeling that I felt was a feeling of dread that the cancer had returned.

"Neesy."

Legend's voice halted all of my movements. I hadn't known he was there but when I looked up and turned towards his voice, I saw that he was sitting right beside me. His face was blank and unreadable so, of course, I figured the worst.

"Legend," I started with tears coming to my eyes. "Just tell me… did it come back? Did the cancer return?"

A glimmer of something passed through his eyes as he shook his head from side-to-side slowly.

"No," he replied back and I let out a sigh of relief. "But…we're going to have a baby. You're pregnant."

Chapter Twenty-Six

LEGEND

"Damn, I can't believe Legend finally knocked somebody up, man. Y'all believe that shit?!" Quan laughed before taking a sip of Crown, straight from the bottle.

"Hell naw, I still don't believe it," Murk grumbled as he held a lit blunt out the side of his mouth. "I wasn't in the room and I didn't hear the doctor say shit, so I ain't buying it."

Leaning over, I draped my arm around Murk's neck and playfully punched him in his chest with my other hand as I laughed.

"Believe it, nigga. My soldiers did what the hell they do. In about eight more months, I'll have my own lil' niggas walkin' around, terrorizing the block."

"What da fuck kinda supersonic muhfuckas you put inside of Neesy?" Quan joked, looking at me with bug-eyes. "If them niggas come out walkin' and shit, I'm tossin' they asses in traffic."

"Don't underestimate a Legend," I chuckled as I pulled from my own blunt. It was stuffed full as hell and bigger than one of my thumbs.

Murk had hooked a nigga up for sure.

"Nigga, stop with all that cocky ass 'Legend' bullshit," Quan shot back, pulling the bottle of Crown from his lips. "You ain't shit but Leith who used to pee in the bed when we were little. I couldn't even sleep at night because you had that plastic shit under the covers on your bed. Every time you turned around, it sounded like plastic bags was fighting or some shit. Peein' in the bed ass nigga!"

"Nigga, I ain't never peed in the fuckin' bed. You confusin' me with your lame ass twin," I told him, snatching the Crown from his hands. "Lay off the Crown, nigga. It's too strong for ya. Got yo' ass misrememberin' shit."

"Yo, you still reading Neesy's textbooks?" Dame asked, looking up from the cup of lean he had in his hands. "Using words like 'misrememberin' now, huh? Don't outgrow ya hood, nigga."

"Y'all ain't shit," I chuckled, pulling from my blunt. "Never gone be shit either."

Life felt good. Matter of fact, it couldn't get better. We were sitting on my favorite spot on the block, Ms. Berneice's steps, laughing, talking, drinking, and smoking, as we celebrated the fact that I had a mini-me on the way. This was the way that I saw my life and how I wanted it to stay. Finally, for once, I was just chilling and didn't have a care in the world.

From time-to-time, I still saw Martinez around, but she stayed in her business and out of my way. From the way that she looked at me, I could tell that she wanted a nigga but she knew there was no hope of anything happening. I had Shanecia and she was all I could ever want.

I was a loyal nigga and that loyalty didn't just extend to my brothers. I was just as loyal to my woman as I was to anyone else, and that would never change.

Every now and then, my mind fell on Elsa and how she'd changed a major part of me. It was crazy how one little lady could pop up in my life in the craziest, most ass backwards way, but change my whole world. She single-handedly convinced me that what I needed in my life was a child of my own and now I finally had exactly what I needed with the only woman I truly loved.

"Nigga, when you gone get a real ring and stop wearing that bubblegum shit you wearing?" Quan asked, pointing at the ring on my finger that Shanecia and I had gotten the day we got married.

Laughing, I raised my hand up and looked at it.

"Never. This is the cheapest shit I've ever worn but it's the only one that's priceless. When my baby buys me another one, I'll take this one off," I told him as I stared at the plastic ring. "We was in a rush and we forgot the rings so we did what we had to do...but I love this."

"Well, yo' baby need to upgrade your ass. That shit is embarrassing as fuck."

"Quan, shut yo' cheap ass up! You probably want him to take it off so you can use it and give it to thickums! Ain't you tired of Legend's hand-me-downs?" Murk piped up, defending me the way he always did.

Snickering to himself, Quan lifted his hands up and shrugged. He began to say something to counter Murk's words, but I was no longer paying attention to him because something in the distance had caught my eye. It was like being hit with a stroke of déjà vu.

"Muthafuckin' Quentin," I muttered as I inhaled my blunt and looked in the distance. "Does he live 'round this bitch or somethin'? How come every time we here, his ass pops up?"

Quan stirred a little as he sat in front of me and my eyes immediately focused on him. His behavior was a dead giveaway. It was obvious he had something to do with this shit.

"I called him," he admitted. "I told him we were here."

"Nigga, why yo' brain-dead ass do some shit like that?" Murk asked, clicking his tongue against his teeth as he glared down at Quan.

"Because he's our brother! Legend, you said that Cush forgives him for what he did! And it wasn't his fault…Gene fucked us all up in different ways! Please, don't keep punishing him for that perverted shit that nigga did to him," Quan pled as he stood up.

With a stone-faced expression, I watched him as Quentin waited in the distance, shifting his footing from left to right nervously. Although Quan's lips had long stopped moving, his eyes were still pleading with me to spare his brother.

My brother.

Our brother.

Maybe it was the fact that I was celebrating a new life and a new beginning with the woman of my dreams. Maybe it was the fact that I'd promised God that I would be a new man. Maybe it was the fact that I was toking on the biggest blunt in history and it had me feeling just that good. Whatever it was, all of a sudden, I found myself nodding my head at Quan.

"You sure?" Quan asked, looking more surprised than I felt.

"Yeah," I said with another curt nod, this time as I looked over at Quentin.

"Well, gotdamn," Murk grunted from beside me. He shifted and turned to look at me with his eyes wide as if he were seeing me for the first time.

"My nigga, you sure you ain't been hit with that mosquito virus that's been goin' 'round? We might need to get your ass checked," he said.

"Naw, I'm good, bro," I assured him with a low chuckle of my own.

I understood where he was coming from though. I had never been the forgiving type. This shit was new to me.

"I already humbled this nigga when I bust him in his shit. We ain't gone have no more problems," I joked and Murk leaned over to give me a dap. I returned it and placed the blunt back between my lips, chiefing hard as I watched Quentin walk towards us.

He looked much different than the way I was used to seeing him. He was definitely calmer, more laid-back, and the wildness in him seemed to be gone. It was obvious that he was still dealing with whatever demons that Gene had caused…hell, we all were. But he seemed to have somewhat of a grip on them.

"Legend, I know how you feel about the shit I've done but I wouldn't have done it if—"

Placing my hand in the air, I signaled him to stop talking. If we were going to mend whatever broken relationship we had, the last thing I wanted him to do was to remind me of the shit he did to Cush. Bringing that up could get him killed because, even though she forgave him, I never could. But because she had forgiven him and because Quan acted like he couldn't live without his fucked up twin by his side, I had to try to let it go.

"Do yourself a favor and don't ever bring up that shit again," I advised him, and he nodded his head.

Turning, I looked at Murk in the eyes, knowing that he wasn't where I was yet. When it came to Quentin, Murk wasn't ready to overlook shit and he damn sure wasn't going to let it go. I didn't expect him to, but I knew that he would respect whatever decision I made.

"Aye, I'mma drop on out of here so I can check on my Li," Murk said, jumping up from where he sat.

Walking around, he gave us all dap, minus Quentin, and then hopped in his ride and drove off in a roar, his tires screeching down the road as he left. When I turned back to Quentin, he had a disappointed look on his face and I knew it was because of Murk, but he was going to have to chuck that one up to the game. Murk was a brother he'd lost and there was no way he would get him back.

"He ain't gone change," I told Quentin, referring to Murk.

"I know it," Quentin replied back honestly.

"But he'll do as I ask him to so, as long as we can come to an agreement, Murk ain't gone say shit about it," I continued.

"I know that, too."

Pausing, I thought about my words as Dame and Quan looked on in astonishment. Thinking about the person I was, I knew why.

I was Legend. The same nigga who didn't have a problem shooting off my guns just for the mere fact that I felt disrespected. I'd done some crazy ass shit…tied up nigga's wives and held them ransom, threatened their kids, dropped in by their mama's house…all shit that I wouldn't hesitate to murder a nigga for if they'd tried it to me. But the situation was different now. I had a wife and a kid on the way. I needed more friends than enemies in these streets. It was no longer just about me.

"We ain't gone never be brothers like how I am with these three," I told Quentin, pointing to Quan and Dame, and the space where Murk had been before he made his exit.

"But, that being said, you're free to stay in the city and you don't gotta worry about me coming after your ass. Just stay the fuck out of my way and I'll stay out of yours. Ya feel me?" I asked, lifting one brow as I watched him intensely and waited for a response.

Massaging his beard with his hand, Quentin paused as he thought about my words. Then suddenly, his face cracked into a wide, goofy ass smile and I swear it seemed like he was showing off all of his damn teeth.

"That's the closest I'mma get to a truce, huh?" he asked, still smiling, and I nodded my head. It was, and I felt damn good about it, even if it wasn't much.

"You want a hit of this?" I asked him as I reached my arm out and held my prized blunt out for him.

His toothy grin spread even wider as he nodded his head and

plucked the blunt from my fingers. I watched as he pulled from it with that same smile plastered on his face, happily and eagerly accepting my peace offering.

"Alright, I'm out this bitch," I told Dame and Quan, reaching out to dap them all up. "I gotta get back to the wife. Damn...that shit still sounds crazy as hell."

Laughing, Dame nodded his head as Quan chuckled and took a long swig of his drink.

"Miracles do happen, nigga," Dame commented as I walked towards the whip.

Nodding my head, I agreed with him.

"That they do."

EPILOGUE

LEGEND

The Birth of a Legend

"One…two…three…PUUUUSSSSSHHHH!"

I watched as Shanecia bit down hard on her bottom lip and grunted, as she pushed with all of her might. She was doing the damn thing, and I couldn't possibly be more in love with her than I was at that moment as she brought forth our child. She'd taken the entire pregnancy like a soldier, but I'd expected it. That's exactly what she was.

"Legeeeeeeennnnddd!" she screamed as she pushed even harder, sweating profusely as she gritted her teeth.

"Yeah?" I asked, confused by why she looked like she wanted to fuck my ass up just for living. Beneath gnashing her teeth and looking at me like I wasn't shit, she pointed her eyes down to her open hand and I realized what she wanted.

"Oh…you could've told me you just wanted to hold on to a

nigga...I can do that—SHIT!" I yelled out when Shanecia grabbed my hand as she went through another contraction. She clamped down on my shit like she was the Incredible Hulk and nearly took my fingers straight off.

"FUCK, Neesy! Let go of my fuckin'—gotdammit!" I shouted, trying to snatch my fingers away. But she had a vice grip on my shit.

"Okay, I can see the head, Shanecia!" the doctor announced, making me feel a rush of excitement that immediately dulled the pain Shanecia was inflicting on me. "Just one more big push!"

I braced myself as I felt Shanecia's grip on my hand tighten.

"Aw hell naw, Neesy! You gone have to let my shit go!" I grumbled as I watched her mentally prepare herself to push on the next contraction.

"C'mon, baby! You can do it. Legend! Stop bein' a punk," Alicia said from the other side of Shanecia's bed.

"Nigga, I don't see yo' ass lending a helpin' muthafuckin' hand! Ah...SHIT!"

And with another mighty squeeze, Shanecia damn near broke all the damn bones in my hand as she gritted her teeth together and pushed for the final time. Wincing, I looked down between her legs and witnessed the most beautiful sight that I'd seen, since the day Shanecia had approached me at the rec center wearing tiny ass shorts and a Spelman shirt, demanding that I stop serving her mama.

"It's a..."

My whole world stopped as I waited for her to tell us what we were having. Honestly, I couldn't even say I had a preference. Shanecia and I had tried twice to find out what the sex of our baby would be, but both times we went to the doctor, our stubborn ass child was turned so that we couldn't tell. After trying twice, we both agreed that we'd just wait. Obviously, our kid wanted to do things on his or her own time.

"Well?!" I said when the doctor paused. "What the hell is it? I'm sittin' in fuckin' suspense here!"

But then she flipped and pulled the baby the rest of the way out and I was able to see for myself. A smile crossed my face as I witnessed my child take in the first gulp of air before letting out an ear-piercing scream.

"It's a boy!"

"My man…" I said as I pulled my hand away from Shanecia's and looked at him.

Bending down, I kissed her on her forehead.

"Thank you," I told her as she cried silently. "Thank you so much for giving me the greatest gift."

Unable to say a word, she went to grab my hand but I snatched my shit away.

"Hell naw, Mighty Joe Young. You done did enough damage already. I'll dap you up but that's it!" I told her with a smile.

"Legend! Stop being so damn rude all the damn time!" Shanecia laughed through her tears as one of the nurses gawked at me. I cut my eyes at her and frowned, making the nurse turn away. She wasn't the one who Shanecia was squeezing the shit out of, but she wanted to judge. She didn't know my pain.

"My grandbaby is so cute!" Alicia sung as she watched the nurses clean him off and inspect all his parts. The doctor handed me the tool to cut the umbilical cord and I did it, feeling a surge of excitement at finally doing something I thought I'd never do. Next, they wrapped him up and laid him against Shanecia's chest. Tears poured down her face as she smiled down at him and showered him with kisses.

"He's so perfect," she cooed as she stared at him.

Now that he was all cleaned up, I walked forward to get a closer look at my lil' man. He had his mother's smooth brown complexion but, other than that, he was all me. Just like I told his ass he better be every time I talked to him while he was chilling in her stomach.

"He looks just like your ass," Shanecia said with a giggle.

"He better…as much as you had me runnin' back and forth to the damn store, fetchin' stuff for your greedy ass."

Reaching out, I ran my finger along his nose and felt an emotion stir in my heart that I'd never felt before. Not even for the few weeks that I thought Elsa was mine. It was hard to explain it but, right then, I knew without a shadow of a doubt that I'd met someone who, after only knowing him for a few minutes, I knew I would die for. Someone I knew I would kill for. It was an unconditional love because he hadn't done a damn thing yet to deserve it, but there it was.

When I looked up from him, I saw Shanecia staring at me, her eyes showing me her understanding of the emotions that I hadn't spoken and barely understood myself.

"You'll be better than me, Junior," I told him as I stroked his hand.

He reached out and grabbed down on my finger hard.

"You got a grip like your mama," I joked, cutting my eyes to Shanecia who rolled her eyes.

"What you wanna name him?" she asked me, lifting one eyebrow. "You said 'Junior' just then but you're a Junior, right? So you wanna call him Leith…the third?"

I crinkled up my nose at her. "Hell naw, because I don't know who the hell Leith Jr. is," I reminded her. She sucked her teeth at me before smiling and shaking her head.

"Right, lil' man?" I said as I smiled down at our son. "Tell yo' mama we don't know who that nigga 'Leith' is…ain't that right, Legend?"

Shanecia rolled her eyes. "You gone call him Legend? For real?"

At the moment, we both looked down at our son who seemed to be going to sleep. But the crazy thing is that, call me crazy, but it looked like he had a smile on his face.

"I ain't gotta call him shit," I told her, looking at the smirk on his face. "He's a Legend. You see what it is."

Shaking her head, Shanecia laughed but then nodded her head. "Legend it is."

"I think I'mma put a different little spin on it though," I added, thinking to myself.

"Oh God…I'm scared," Shanecia replied.

"Okay," a nurse said as she walked up to us. "You want to try feeding him for the first time?"

Since Shanecia had only had surgery on one of her breasts in order to remove the cancer, she was still able to breastfeed from the other. I was happy for her because I knew how she felt about breastfeeding and it was important to her to be able to do it for our child.

Stepping back, I shot them all the deuces.

"I don't need to see this part," I announced as I stepped towards the sink to clean up. "Y'all make it do what it do to make sure my lil' man full. I'll be right back."

"Legend ain't got no damn sense," Alicia scoffed as I walked out.

When I got in the hallway, Murk was already standing there holding out a blunt. Next to him was Maliah with her arms crossed in front of her chest and a crazy look on her face. When I saw what Murk was holding, I knew why she had the screwface on.

"I know you need this shit…I done gone through what your ass just went through before," he said, wearing a serious expression on his face.

"You gotta excuse your brother," Maliah said. "But I'm sure you know he don't have no type of fuckin' home training."

Laughing, I batted Murk's hand away. "I'm good but good looking out, man."

"UNCLE L!" Elsa's voice chimed out from down the hall.

I turned around and saw her running towards me with her hands in the air, one holding that damn doll. Dame was right behind her, walking towards me with Quan, and Quentin a little behind him.

Although I was against the idea at first, Quan and Dame convinced me to bring Quentin into the fold and it had been a good idea…especially since I'd pretty much removed myself from the dope game, as I'd promised God when Shanecia was in surgery.

The D-Boys still needed to own the streets, even with me not running them like I used to, and Quentin was happy to do the job. In time, I realized that I needed my brothers. All of them. Murk was beginning to realize that, too, which was a surprise. He didn't fuck with Quentin like he did me, Quan and Dame, but he at least got used to him being around and treated him with respect. I had hope that one day he'd fully come around.

"Elsa, I'mma leave you with Aunty Li, okay?" I told her and she nodded her head then gave me a tight hug.

Placing her down on the floor, I ruffled her hair and smiled when she frowned at me. She wasn't mine but I loved the shit out of my niece.

"Y'all got your pieces on you?" I asked my brothers.

"Fa'sho. It was a boy?" Murk asked, lifting one eyebrow.

I smiled and nodded my head. "Sho' was…so you already know what it is."

"Yes, indeed."

"Well, let's do this shit!" Dame exclaimed, taking his gun out before we even got outside. All I could do was laugh at how excited he was. We all were. We had another little Dumas nigga to add to our legacy.

We scaled the hospital stairs until we found an exit to the roof and walked outside. We could see the city. Our city. In our minds, we were on top of the world.

And then, with our hands held high, we lifted our pistols up and let off a shot to celebrate the most recent addition into the Dumas clan: King Legend Dumas.

THE END!

I am playing with the idea of doing a spin-off on Maliah & Murk…it will be available to the subscribers of my upcoming app *FIRST* before it hits Amazon.

SO TEXT *GETLIT* TO *22828* TO JOIN THE MAILING LIST FOR THE APP SO YOU'LL BE THE FIRST TO KNOW!

MAKE SURE TO LEAVE A REVIEW!

Text PORSCHA to 25827
to keep up with Porscha's latest releases!

To find out more about her, visit www.porschasterling.com

Join our mailing list to get a notification when Leo Sullivan Presents has another release!
Text **LEOSULLIVAN** to **22828** to join!

To submit a manuscript for our review, email us at <u>leosullivanpresents@gmail.com</u>

THANKS FROM PORSCHA STERLING

I'm totally in love with these characters and so sad to see them go but I'm glad they all got their happy ending (and I hope you are, too!).

I want to thank Leo Sullivan for believing in me enough to present me as an author, as well as this series! You're the best and God couldn't have given me a better mentor! Thank you so much for everything that you do!

Special thanks to the greatest editor I could ask for, Latisha Burns, you went waaayyyy beyond the call of duty with this one! Not only did you edit the series to perfection but you listened to me cry about what these crazy characters were putting me through. You always push me to deliver and we get it done together!

Thank you to Quiana Nicole for holding it down like only you can while I got lost in writing this series! You're a great partner, a beautiful person and an amazing friend. I pride myself on not keeping "Yes Men" in my corner and you are DEFINITELY not that!

Thank you #Royalty! We have some of the best authors on the planet! You all R-O-C-K! Keep writing those #DopeBooks!

To the readers – I do it all for you! As long as you all keep reading, I'll keep writing. Even if you aren't reading, I'll still write because it's what I do!

Last but not least, to my favorite person, Alphonzo! Mommy loves you! It's always been and will always be FOR YOU!

Get ready because MY NEXT SERIES IS COMING SOON!

Please make sure to leave a review! I love reading them!I would love it if you reach out to me on Facebook, Instagram or Twitter!

Also, join my Facebook group! I love to interact with my readers. If you haven't already, text PORSCHA to 25827 to join my text list. Text ROYALTY to 42828 to join our email list and read excerpts and learn about giveaways.

Peace, love & blessings to everyone. I love allllll of you!

Porscha Sterling

CPSIA information can be obtained
at www.ICGtesting.com
Printed in the USA
LVHW050452030322
712449LV00004B/192